Agent Matt Christensen could save her life this Christmas.

If he didn't kill her first, that is. After all, she'd broken into the home of a federal agent. Not the safest thing she had ever done.

Outside, she could hear the icy December wind assaulting the trees and Agent Christensen entering through his mudroom. Cass listened as he made his way to the b........ on some music........ ootsteps on th.....

She cr.......... ... the only so........ ....ng rhythm of a bluesy saxophonist whining out a familiar Christmas carol. Sax music and Dean Koontz paperbacks scattered everywhere. Under different circumstances, she might have wondered what else they had in common.

She eased the door open just a fraction.

And met Matt Christensen.

Or rather she met the barrel of his gun.

CAST OF CHARACTERS

Special Agent Matt Christensen – He had no idea that his late estranged lover had given birth to his child, or that the child had been illegally adopted by a notorious crime lord. But once Matt learns he's a father, he joins forces with Cass Harrison to risk everything to rescue his baby.

Cass Harrison – The Texas heiress has been on the run for a year. She's counting on Matt to help her find the evidence to clear her name.

Molly Christensen – Matt's six-month-old daughter. She's too young to know that Cass and her daddy are risking their lives to rescue her.

Ronald McKenzie – Matt's friend and fellow agent who agrees to help rescue Molly.

Dominic Cordova – In addition to having Matt's daughter, the crime lord also framed Cass for murder.

Annette Cordova – Dominic's wheelchair-bound sister, who would do anything to keep Molly, the child she and her brother illegally adopted.

Libby Rayburn – A federal agent who claims she wants to help Matt and Cass.

Hollis Beckman – The secretive groundskeeper at Dominic's estate.

Gideon Tate – Matt's boss. He's following departmental orders, which prevent him from arresting Dominic.

Collena Drake – The troubled former cop who now devotes her life to finding dozens of illegally adopted babies.

The Christmas Clue

DELORES FOSSEN

MILLS & BOON

Pure reading pleasure

*All the characters in this book have no existence outside the
imagination of the author, and have no relation whatsoever to anyone
bearing the same name or names. They are not even distantly inspired
by any individual known or unknown to the author, and all the
incidents are pure invention.*

*First published in Great Britain 2008
by Harlequin Mills & Boon Limited,
Eton House, 18-24 Paradise Road, Richmond, Surrey TW9 1SR*

© Delores Fossen 2007

ISBN: 978 0 263 86005 4

46-1108

*Harlequin Mills & Boon policy is to use papers that are
natural, renewable and recyclable products and made from
wood grown in sustainable forests. The logging and
manufacturing processes conform to the legal environmental
regulations of the country of origin.*

*Printed and bound in Spain
by Litografia Rosés S.A., Barcelona*

ABOUT THE AUTHOR

Imagine a family tree that includes Texas cowboys, Choctaw and Cherokee Indians, a Louisiana pirate and a Scottish rebel who battled side by side with William Wallace. With ancestors like that, it's easy to understand why Texas author and former air force captain Delores Fossen feels as if she was genetically predisposed to writing romances. Along the way to fulfilling her DNA destiny, Delores married an air force top gun who just happens to be of Viking descent. With all those romantic bases covered, she doesn't have to look too far for inspiration.

To Beth.
Thank you for just being you.

Chapter One

Cibolo, Texas

Cass Harrison tightened her grip on the tranquilizer gun and waited.

Her heartbeat pounded in her ears, and she could feel every nerve in her body. She wanted to get out of there fast. But she couldn't. Because this confrontation was the first step.

And because Agent Matt Christensen could save her life.

If he didn't kill her first, that is.

After all, she'd broken into the home of a federal agent. Not the safest thing she had ever done. Hopefully, it would be worth the risk.

Standing at the window of his dining room, Cass made another check of the massive backyard so she could reassure herself one more time that she hadn't been followed. It seemed clear. She prayed it would stay that way.

Outside, she could hear the icy December wind assault the trees. No traffic noise, though. Agent Christensen's house was only twenty minutes from San Antonio, but there were no signs of the city here. His white limestone lodge-style house was nestled in the center of five heavily wooded acres, a location that had been a blessing and a curse. The seclusion had allowed her to leave her car a mile away on a nearly deserted side street and sneak into the house sight unseen. But the semi-isolation meant there'd be no one to help if something went wrong.

She was literally on her own.

Of course, it'd been that way for months now.

"Thank you," Cass mumbled when she finally heard the cue that she'd been waiting for—the metallic grind of the garage door opening, then the sound of Agent Christensen entering through his mudroom.

There was a rustle of movement, and Cass listened as he made his way to the other side of the house. To his bedroom, where he would hopefully take off his standard-issue semiautomatic so it wouldn't be readily available for him to try to use on her. He turned on some music. Not loud. But maybe loud enough to muffle her footsteps on the hardwood floors.

Before she could change her mind, Cass slipped out of the dining room and into the tiny kitchen. Keeping close to the wall, she went into the hall and toward his bedroom. She tried not to think of what might happen once she confronted him.

Maybe he would listen to her. *Maybe.*

And if he didn't…well, Cass had studied what she could access of his official records, and at six-foot-two and one-hundred-and-ninety pounds, Agent Matt Christensen could easily pulverize her.

Forcing that unsettling thought aside, Cass inched toward his bedroom. The only sounds were the steady pulsing rhythm of a bluesy saxophonist whining a familiar Christmas carol. Sax music and Dean Koontz paperbacks scattered all over the house. Under different circumstances, she might have wondered what else Matt Christensen and she had in common.

After a mumbled prayer, she eased open the door. Just a fraction.

And came face-to-face with Matt Christensen.

Or rather with the gun he stuck right in her face.

Cass nearly screamed from the surprise, but she tamped down any startled response and kept a firm grip on her own weapon, such that it was. Not easy to manage with her suddenly trembling hands. And, mercy, her knees were shaking.

Despite all her trembling and shaking, she had no trouble seeing the man behind that gun. Matt Christensen wore black pants and a white shirt that he'd unbuttoned.

He looked one hundred percent lethal.

His bio had been dead-on. He was formidable, and his pretty-boy looks didn't diminish that. He was blond-haired, blue-eyed, toned and naturally tanned.

And because his shirt was open, she could also see that he had muscled pecs and abs.

Even though he was a prime specimen of a man, Cass didn't dare let that distract her. Not a chance. This situation could easily get out of hand even more than it already was.

"Well?" he said.

Definitely not a greeting but more like a challenge. It also had a tinge of a Texas drawl and more than a bit of dismissal to it. If he were even remotely concerned about having an armed intruder walk in on him, he didn't show it.

"I need to talk to you," Cass managed to say.

He lifted his left eyebrow. "And you thought aiming a tranquilizer gun at me was the easiest way to do that?"

"The safest," she corrected. "I'm not here to hurt you, only to talk. I couldn't meet with you at your office. Not with their security measures. And the office, assignments, your city apartment and this house seem to be the only places you ever go. You really don't have much of a life," she added in a mumble.

"I suppose this is your idea of getting me a life?"

"In a way. Just think of this as an early Christmas present." Cass backed out into the hallway, to put some physical distance between them. It didn't help. Matt Christensen still seemed to be right in her face.

"How did you get into my house?" he asked.

"I picked the lock. It's a little skill that I've unfortunately had to learn to stay alive. It also helped that your security system wasn't on. I guess this isn't a high crime area out here. By the way, I'm Cass Harrison—"

"Even with the dye job and the bad haircut, I know who you are," he interrupted. "Cassandra Leeann Harrison. Age twenty-eight. Last known residence, San Antonio. I've seen your pictures at least a dozen times in the newspapers and on wanted flyers."

She resisted the urge to try to smooth her fingers through what he considered her bad cut. And it *was* bad. Being on the run from the authorities didn't leave much time for visits to the hair salon.

"You're an heiress. Or at least you used to be. Now, you're a rich fugitive from justice," he continued. "I know of at least two federal agencies who want to question you."

"What they want is to put me in prison for something I didn't do."

"You didn't assist your former boyfriend, Dominic Cordova, with his illegal transfer of funds to a South American bank account? And you didn't murder his business associate when he discovered that illegal transfer?"

There it was. The accusations in a nutshell. A simple cockily delivered summary of something that hadn't been so simple. It'd been earth-shattering, life altering. It'd felt as if someone had crushed her heart.

"No." Cass shook her head. "I didn't have any idea

Dominic would set me up to take the fall for those charges. But it doesn't matter now. All that matters is I finally get to clear my name, and you're going to help me do it."

He rolled those deep blue eyes. "I have no intention of helping you evade these charges."

"I think you will, once you hear what I have to say. I believe there's evidence at Dominic Cordova's estate in West Texas that will exonerate me."

"So?" he challenged.

"So, the Justice Department has put Dominic off-limits." It wasn't a guess, either. Cass had kept very close tabs on Dominic, and she didn't care much for the authorities' change in attitude toward him.

"Political alliances make strange bedfellows," Christensen countered. "The department considers you the bad guy, Ms. Harrison. Not Dominic Cordova. These days, he's the man they're backing to help them bring down criminals that they consider to be a lot worse."

"There isn't anyone worse than Dominic. And as I said, there's evidence at his estate that'll prove that the Justice Department can't trust him. I want you to use your training and your contacts to help me get that evidence."

His mouth quivered, threatening to smile. "I'm a federal agent, not a mercenary. Nor an idiot."

"I don't trust idiots or mercenaries. I've been burned by a few of the latter who've tried to sell me out for the bounty that Dominic has on my head."

"But you'd trust me?" he fired back.

She huffed, and made sure it conveyed "not on your life."

Matt Christensen huffed, too. "Let's get something straight, lady. I'm not going to risk my career, my butt or anything else to help you. In fact, I'm going to call the cops so they can come and get you."

"You can't call them." Cass raced after him, caught on his arm and somehow managed to get him to stop. Touching practically every part of his body, she squeezed past him and into the corridor just off the kitchen so she could step in front of him and meet his gaze head-on.

"Just listen to me," she bargained. "And at the end of my explanation, if you still want to call the police, then I won't stop you."

It was a massive lie. A necessary one designed to buy her some time. She *would* stop him. Someway, somehow. Because an arrest would almost certainly lead to her death. Dominic or one of his hired guns would see to it that she wasn't around to accuse him of the things he'd done. In the eleven-and-a-half months she'd been on the run, there'd been almost a half-dozen attempts on her life. In prison she'd be a sitting duck.

Matt Christensen studied her a moment with eyes that were somehow sizzling and cool at the same time. It wasn't a quick assessment. In the depths of all those shades of blue, Cass could see the battle he was having with himself. A battle about whether or not to listen.

"Start talking," he ordered.

Cass knew a gift when she saw it, and she didn't waste time. "For months I've been trying to figure out how to prove I'm innocent. I finally got a break from an unexpected source, a former cop named Collena Drake. The police busted an illegal adoption ring, and she's been going through hundreds of files related to the case. I heard through the grapevine that she'd seen Dominic's name as an adopter."

"And this is somehow linked to the evidence that'll exonerate you?" He couldn't have possibly sounded more disinterested.

Cass nodded and suddenly wished she'd rehearsed this. "Look, what I'm about to tell you might be a little…shocking."

He stared at her.

"Right," Cass concluded. "You're not easily shocked." She took a deep breath. "Okay, here goes. I called Collena Drake, and I pretended to be a servant at Dominic's estate. I said I was concerned about a child that Dominic had recently adopted. Ms. Drake confirmed that Dominic had indeed adopted one of the babies in question. She'd yet to confirm that the process was illegal, but it was highly suspect. Because, believe me, Dominic wouldn't qualify for a normal adoption. There are all kinds of skeletons dangling in his closet."

"A baby," he repeated. He shrugged. A dismissal sort of gesture that wasn't as effective as his other brash expressions. Because while his shoulder might have

been shrugging off her question, his eyes were de-
manding more info. "Why would you bring this to me?
If you think the adoption was illegal, you should be in-
forming the police."

Oh, this was about to get messy. Very messy.
"Remember Vanessa Jordan?"

Matt Christensen blinked. "Yeah. Of course, I do.
It'd be hard to forget my ex-girlfriend. She's dead. And
what could she possibly have to do with you or this
visit?"

Cass knew that the woman had everything to do
with it. "You didn't stay in contact after she broke off
things with you."

"No. And it was by mutual agreement."

She braced herself to deliver what he wasn't going
to want to hear. "Vanessa had a baby six months ago.
She gave birth the day she died."

Another shrug, and it was even less effective than
the last one. But then, it had to be. The ice man routine
wouldn't stand a chance against news like that. He
pinned his narrowed gaze to hers. "You believe
Vanessa's baby was part of this illegal adoption ring?"

"Yes. And more. Let's do the math. Thirteen months
ago, Vanessa and you broke up. Then, she gave birth
seven months later."

Matt Christensen mumbled some profanity under his
breath. Really bad profanity that didn't seem to be
steeped in surprise or anger. It all seemed to be aimed
at her.

"Okay, let's do some more math," he commented. He casually propped his shoulder against the wall and angled his body so they were directly facing each other again. "Vanessa could have gotten pregnant right after we broke up, and then she could have delivered a preemie. It happens all the time."

"Yes. But according to the records that Collena Drake found, the baby weighed over eight pounds when she was born. Hardly the birth weight of a preemie."

"What are you saying?" Christensen snapped. But he didn't wait for Cass to answer. "That the child is mine? No way in hell, because Vanessa was on the pill the whole time we were together. And we were careful because neither of us was ready to become parents."

Since there was probably nothing she could say that would convince him, Cass decided it was time for the more direct, visual-aid approach. She motioned toward the pocket of her brown leather jacket. "I'm going to reach inside, so don't shoot first and assume I'm going for a real gun."

Only after he nodded—a gesture laced with reluctance and more of that cocky attitude—Cass slipped her hand inside and took out the picture. A picture that had not been easy to obtain. She'd had to pay off Dominic's head groundskeeper to use a camera with a long-range lens.

"Vanessa was a redhead. Like me, before the dye job and the bad haircut. She also had green eyes. A Scots-

Irish-dominated gene pool." She aimed her index finger at him. "Then, there's you. If you introduced yourself as Thor Svenson and claimed you were of Viking descent, people would believe you in a heartbeat."

With that, she handed him the photograph, and after more of that mumbled profanity, he took it.

Cass watched as his suspicious gaze eased away from hers and skimmed over the round-faced baby sitting in a stroller in a garden. But soon the skimming stopped, and his attention speared on to that image.

In the photograph, the angle of the sun was just right so that it glistened off the child's loose curls that haloed around her head.

Blond curls.

And coupled with the little girl's clearly visible piercing blue eyes, Cass figured that Matt Christensen wouldn't be shrugging again anytime soon.

This wasn't something he could shrug off.

Because he'd no doubt just realized that he was looking at the face of a child he hadn't even known existed.

His baby daughter.

Chapter Two

Matt stared at the photo, and he stared at it some more. Even though he tried to tamp down all the wild scenarios that started to fly through his head, he wasn't completely successful. The little girl was a dead ringer for him.

"You're a fugitive from justice," he pointed out, talking just as much to himself as his breaking-and-entering visitor. "So, why I should believe anything you say?"

"Because I'm telling the truth."

No hesitation. None. It still didn't help convince him otherwise, and she obviously realized that, from the Arctic look he gave her.

"The truth?" he questioned, upping that icy look a notch. He handed her back the photo, and she put it in her pocket. "I doubt it. You probably had the picture doctored. Or maybe that wasn't even necessary. Maybe you just found some kid who looks like me and decided to use her to run this…whatever this is."

She looked genuinely insulted. "Why would I make up something like that?"

"Easy. To convince me to help you get this so-called evidence from Dominic Cordova's estate."

That earned him a glare. And she was good at it, too. Those cat-green eyes could slice, dice and dismiss all in the same glance.

"Then, if you follow that through to its logical conclusion," she countered, "I must be telling you the truth about there being evidence to exonerate me. Or else why would I need your help?" She paused, and let that hum between them for a few seconds. "Now, do me a favor and take that even one step further. If I'm telling the truth about that, then I'm also telling the truth about the little girl in that picture. She's your daughter."

Matt shook his head. "There's nothing logical about that conclusion."

And that meant he had to figure out the next step. He could just call the cops and have her arrested. One call. A simple solution. He could have her out of his house within twenty minutes. Maybe less. But his instincts told him to take a little detour first. Not that it would change the outcome. Not that it would prevent her arrest, but it'd make him sleep a little easier if he confirmed, or disproved, a few things.

First things first though. He reached out and grabbed her tranquilizer gun. He definitely surprised her, because judging from the look on her face, she had no idea it was coming. Only after he'd successfully disarmed her did Matt take his cell phone from his pocket.

"No!" she practically yelled. She grabbed him, clamping onto his arm and shoving him against the wall. "I can't let you call the cops."

He actually had to bite back a smile. The woman had courage.

Or *something*.

Maybe desperation was the great equalizer because he towered over her and outweighed her by a good seventy pounds, and still she tried to hang on to him. While they were practically plastered against each other.

She noticed that, too.

Her gaze slipped from his eyes and landed on his right thigh and groin that pressed against her jeans. With her free hand, she reached down and gave his thigh a shove, which was a necessary adjustment. Unfortunately, her hand wasn't too steady, or else she wanted to torture him. Because her touch was more of a grope, and she almost gave him an erection in the process. It was surefire reminder that it'd been a while since he'd been this close to a woman.

"Why don't we take this conversation out of this narrow hallway so we're not practically standing on top of each other?" she suggested. "And then we can discuss why you can't call the police."

"I'm not calling them," he informed her. *"Yet."*

"Then who?"

"A friend. And I don't plan on telling him you're here. As far as I'm concerned, you're my problem, not his. I just want some information." And Matt didn't want to try to get that info while trying to keep an eye on his visitor.

She waited a moment, staring at him. "What's your definition of a friend?"

Matt decided to keep things vague. "Someone who can prove you're lying."

"Oh." And she actually relaxed a little.

A reaction that had Matt tensing a lot. It couldn't be possible. Cass Harrison couldn't be telling the truth.

"This call would be to someone we both can trust?" she asked. "By that, I mean to someone not in the Justice Department."

Again, he kept things vague. "The call will be safe."

She released the grip she had on his arm, took a step back and motioned for him to continue. Matt took her up on that—after he continued to consider her response and then dismissed it as some bizarre mind game.

Yes, that had to be it.

He made the call. To his friend and co-worker, Agent Ronald McKenzie. Definitely someone in the Justice Department. He didn't have the same reservations about safety that Cass did.

"Ronald," Matt greeted. He winced when he heard Ronald give a groggy yawn. It was past 10:00 p.m. and obviously bedtime for some. "Sorry to wake you, but this is an emergency of sorts. I need you to run something on our old pal, Dominic Cordova. I'd like to know if he's become a father in the past six months."

That stopped Ronald in midyawn. "A father?"

It wasn't just a simple question. Ronald wanted to know what had precipitated this call. But Matt didn't want to get into that yet. So he trimmed down the details of an explanation and hoped it would suffice. "Yeah. I've heard rumors that he adopted a child." He paused, because he had to. "I've also heard rumors that this baby might have a connection to Vanessa."

"You're kidding?"

"Nope. But like I said, it's probably just a rumor." Or an out-and-out lie.

"I'll check," Ronald promised. "And then I'll call you right back."

"Thanks."

Matt pushed the end call button, slipped the phone into his pocket and looked at her. Her face wasn't hard to miss since she was right there in front of him. They were practically standing on each other. Way too close. It was time to do something about that, so Matt stepped around her. Unfortunately, his arm swiped her right breast, causing her to suck in her breath. Matt ignored both the swipe and her reaction, and he headed into the kitchen, figuring she'd follow.

She did.

"Too bad you're not a Navy SEAL," she mumbled. She brushed her fingers over the tiny one-foot mini tree that had come predecorated with about a dozen tacky ornaments. It was his sole attempt to recognize the holidays. "I hear they're fearless."

Matt just glared at her. "That won't work."

"What won't?" she asked innocently.

"Insulting me."

She scratched her eyebrow. Auburn eyebrows that didn't match her now-chocolate-brown hair. "I was actually trying to goad you."

"That won't work, either. So, talk to me about this so-called evidence that'll exonerate you," Matt insisted. If there was anything to it, and that was a huge *if,* he could pass on the info to the authorities once she was in custody.

"Surveillance disks," she answered. "Dominic records everything that goes on in every room. And I mean *everything.* Since the murder happened in his office at the estate, I'm sure some information about it will be on one or more of the disks."

Matt didn't even try to suppress a loud groan. "And I'm guessing there are plenty of these disks?"

"Hundreds in a vault in the basement. I have the code to get into the vault. That's not the problem. The problem is, according to someone who's familiar with the estate, Dominic only keeps each disk one year. That means if I don't act fast, he'll erase any evidence I can use."

He leaned slightly closer. "That isn't helping your case, you know."

"You mean because if Dominic records everything,

then the sheer volume will make it impossible for us to find the evidence?"

"*You,*" he corrected.

"*You* what?"

"You said it'll be impossible for *us* to find the evidence. There is no *us* in this delusional plan, only *you.*"

"Oh, there's an *us* all right." She shook her head, and sent a lock of her chin-length hair sliding across her cheekbone. "The little blond-haired girl in that picture changes everything."

"No. She doesn't."

And Matt was *almost* positive he believed that.

Cass Harrison apparently thought otherwise because she just stared at him.

"Okay," he said trying a different angle. "Let's suppose for argument's sake that there is disk evidence. How do you intend to get it?"

"*We* will use equipment to jam Dominic's disk surveillance feed. After that, we can gain access to the basement. Since covert measures are your specialty, that shouldn't be a problem. Then, we'll open the vault and search through the disks until we find what we're looking for."

Matt bypassed the last half of what she said and groaned again. "Equipment? What kind of equipment?"

"That's another area where I'll need your help. I don't have access to the kind of equipment necessary to bypass Dominic's state-of-the-art security system, and it's not something I can buy."

Matt really didn't like the direction this conversation was taking. "But I do have access?"

She made an *of course* sound. "Don't make me quote questionably obtained intel reports about the recent rescue of an American businesswoman who was being held hostage in South America. The only way the military and the Justice Department could have gotten her out was if they'd used the exact kind of jamming equipment that we need."

He scowled at her. "And you think the Justice Department just leaves this equipment unsecured so anyone can use it?"

"No. But I think you can get it if it becomes necessary. And guess what? That little girl in the picture makes it necessary."

Matt leaned in. "Yet another example of totally faulty reasoning. Or maybe it's just a lie."

She groaned. "I wish you'd stop accusing me of lying."

"Sorry." An apology Matt definitely didn't mean, and his tone conveyed that. "It's just that I get a little testy when someone breaks into my house, holds a tranquilizer gun on me and then demands that I steal classified equipment, break ranks and join in a half-assed, stupid plan that would almost certainly get both of us killed."

"It's not a half-assed, stupid plan." But then she

paused, shrugged. "Okay, maybe it does have some half-assed, stupid elements to it, but I'm doing the best I can with what I have. And what I have is *you,* Matt Christensen. You're a highly trained federal agent. You can get us into that estate."

In most cases, that would be true.

But not this time.

Judging from the intel reports he'd read, Dominic Cordova's estate was a fortress. With reason. The man had enraged at least a dozen people, criminals, who killed as easily as they breathed. And that kind of situation made a person paranoid about security.

"Why didn't you just ask the authorities to check out Dominic's place, huh?" Matt asked. "If the evidence is there, they could find it—legally."

"First of all, the authorities wouldn't believe me. And if by some miracle they did, they wouldn't risk offending their new ally by requesting the necessary documents to do a search of his estate. Plus, I'm about ninety-nine percent sure there's a leak in communications. I think Dominic may have an insider in the Justice Department, and this person might be feeding him official information."

Interesting. Matt hadn't heard that particular accusation. Perhaps because she'd just made it up. He certainly wasn't about to assume it was true. "Is that a guess, or do you actually have proof?"

"Proof. I did a test a few days ago and phoned in some bogus info to a person I thought I could trust in the Justice Department. Then, I timed it. In less than an hour, Dominic received a call on his secure line at his estate. The caller spoke through a computer voice scrambler so I have no idea who he or she is, but the person relayed the bogus info verbatim to Dominic."

Matt considered all of that and decided it could mean nothing. It did, however, warrant some further investigating. "Do I dare ask how you gained access to Dominic's secure phone line?"

"No." She had the decency to look slightly embarrassed. "That's not a good question to ask."

If this entire conversation hadn't been so frustrating, Matt would have smiled. But he doubted he'd be doing much smiling tonight. "How'd you ever hook up with Dominic Cordova in the first place?"

She angled her head and stared at him. "Is this small talk?"

"In a way." Matt checked his watch. "I'm waiting on my friend to call back. If he doesn't within the next ten minutes, I'm phoning the cops. I figure this is as good a way as any to pass the time."

For a moment Matt didn't think she'd answer. Strange, since she'd volunteered everything else. But then, he'd probably riled her with that threat to call the cops. Which wasn't exactly a threat. He *would* call them.

As soon as Ronald verified that she was lying.

"Dominic," she mumbled, saying his name as if it were a persistent infection. She thumped a tiny Santa figure dangling from the Christmas plant and sent the Santa swaying. "He sought me out, attending the same parties, the same social functions. He pursued me. At the time, I didn't realize it was a setup, that he wasn't interested in me nearly as much as my multimillion-dollar trust fund."

"He's that good an actor?"

Her sigh was laced with regret. "He's that good, and I can usually spot a phony. My parents might have been wealthy, but they weren't born that way. They were streetwise, and before they died they were always warning me about guys like Dominic."

"But you missed the signs with him," he pointed out.

"Obviously."

She quickly looked away after her gaze landed on his bare chest, making him wish he'd taken the time to rebutton his shirt after he'd realized he had an intruder in the house. This was not good. Even with all the unreasonable demands, Cass Harrison was still a woman.

An attractive woman who had a unique way of re-minding him that he was a man.

"I missed the signs because I was thinking with the wrong part of my body," she explained. "It took me seven weeks to realize that Dominic wanted to use my money and business contacts to carry out illegal ac-tivities."

Matt didn't doubt that part, but he also believed that Cass had loved getting involved with a dangerous man.

It was what bored socialites like her did. And he should know. Vanessa had done the same thing to him.

She'd loved his job. The danger of it. The excitement. It'd gotten her hot. But that heat had fizzled out very quickly when she grew bored with him and his lack of massive amounts of money.

That was something he had to accept. And it was a realization that still caused Matt to curse himself for ever getting involved with a blue-blood heiress in the first place. At least it was a lesson learned.

And one he wouldn't repeat.

Ever.

Even if the heiress across from him was causing him to have a few lustful thoughts.

Cass pulled in a hard breath and stood. "You're not going to help me, are you?"

"No."

She slipped her hands into the back pockets of her well-worn jeans. It was a little maneuver that had her navy blue sweater tightening across her breasts and hitching up to expose an inch or two of her stomach. No bra. And how did he know that? Because the sides of her jacket were far enough apart that he could see the outline of her erect nipples.

Oh, man.

Why didn't he just hit himself in the head? He shouldn't be looking at her. She was as off-limits as any woman could possibly be. When this was over, he really did need to take some time and get laid.

"I can't recover the evidence on my own," she said, her voice a little quavery now. More than quavery. Feminine. Not good. That quavery feminine voice teased his protective instincts while her semibare midriff teased a part of him that needed no such teasing. "And if I do nothing, I have to stay on the run. Not exactly how I want to spend the rest of my life."

He made a grunt of agreement and forced his attention away from that snug sweater. "You know the old saying about being between a rock and a hard place. Guess that's where you are right now."

She made a mimicking grunt of agreement, and while the sound was still reverberating in her throat, she pulled her right hand from behind her. Not slowly, either. She was fast. Damn fast. And her hand wasn't empty, either.

She aimed a gun—a real gun—right at him. "I always carry backup," she let him know.

"Hell," he mumbled, and he silently chastised himself with some much-stronger profanity. How had he let the situation come to this?

Oh, wait.

He knew what had caused his lapse in judgment. It was her nipple-showing sweater and that quavery voice. He'd stupidly let them distract him, and now that stupidity might have some serious consequences.

Matt glanced at her and then took a better look at her weapon. He instantly recognized the model. A Kahr PM9. A trim 9 mm with a tiny three-inch barrel. Heck, the whole gun was only five inches long, so no wonder he hadn't noticed it in what was no doubt a slide holster tucked in the back waist of her jeans. But Matt knew this was a case where size truly didn't matter. It was a combat weapon and just as deadly as any gun in the wrong hands could be.

"This is a mistake," he insisted. Not his best attempt at reasoning, but Matt was still berating himself for allowing the situation to escalate into this.

"A mistake? I don't think so. I have a different saying for you—a woman's place is behind the trigger. Guess *that's* where I am right now."

Man, she was as good with the wise comebacks as she was at distracting him. Too bad he'd have to be the one to make sure she was arrested. And it was really too bad that he didn't like having to do that. It was his job to protect and defend, he reminded himself. But a part of him, a very small part of him, wouldn't have minded if Cass Harrison had somehow been able to find evidence to clear her name. Especially since that would send Dominic to jail for the rest of his life.

"So, what now?" Matt asked her. "I'm your hostage?"

She nodded. "Temporarily. Take off your pants."

He lifted an eyebrow. "You're going to sexually assault me?"

That earned him one of those glares and a nasty little huff. "You wish. I'll use them to tie you up. I don't especially want to go rifling around your place to find something to restrain you."

Oh, so she did have a plan.

Such that it was.

Matt unzipped his pants, all the while looking for the opportunity to disarm her. It wouldn't take much. Just a split-second distraction, and then he could launch himself at her. A tackle of sorts. And then he would call the authorities. Her time was up.

Stripped down to his shirt and boxer briefs, he extended his arm in front of him and dropped his pants on the kitchen floor.

In the three feet of space that separated them.

She scowled, probably because she knew it would be a major mistake to try to reach down and pick them up. Instead, she kept her gaze fastened on him and used her foot to drag the pants closer to her. She didn't stop there. Cass began to back up, moving farther away from him.

The sound of the phone ringing sliced through the room. It was exactly the distraction he'd been waiting for. She automatically glanced at the phone mounted to the wall, and that glance cost her.

Matt launched himself at her.

She didn't fire. In fact, she didn't even attempt to shoot him. She turned, as if to run, but Matt latched on to her shoulder. His full weight slammed into her, and the momentum sent them both crashing to the floor. They landed between a pair of bar stools.

Somewhere amid the sounds of the struggle, he heard his answering machine kick it. "It's Matt. Leave a message."

Matt relied on his training. He turned, maneuvered and adjusted until he had her pinned down, and then he wrenched the small gun from her hand. Because her knee could quickly become a painful weapon, he literally pressed her entire body against the floor so she couldn't move.

"Matt, are you there?" Agent Ronald McKenzie said into the answering machine. It was a call that Matt would have liked to answer, but there was no way he would let go of Cass now that he'd subdued her. Well, sort of.

He might have gotten her physically restrained, but she was hurling eye daggers at him and was mumbling some rather creative profanity through bursts of labored breath. It was obvious she wouldn't give up and was probably already looking for another way to escape.

"I checked on our *friend* for you," he heard Ronald say. "I found something."

Matt couldn't help it. That comment captured his complete attention. It obviously captured Cass's, too, because she stilled, her body practically going limp, and her gaze drifted in the direction of the phone.

"Just asking the question seemed to make a few people uncomfortable," Ronald explained, his voice noticeably laced with anxiety. "Still, I asked, and here's the answer I got—it appears that six months ago Dominic Cordova did indeed adopt a baby. He named the girl Molly."

Matt felt as if someone had slugged him.

Oh, man.

All he could do was lie there while Ronald continued.

"I hope I'm wrong, but I doubt it, so here goes. The adoption might not have been aboveboard. It's all tied to that illegal adoption ring that the San Antonio PD recently broke up. And if you're thinking this kid belongs to Vanessa, you're right. The timing is dead-on. Vanessa did have a baby, and Dominic's adopted child was born in the very hospital and at the very minute that Vanessa gave birth. But here's the clincher, and believe me, it's not a clincher you're going to like."

Matt looked down at Cass at the exact moment she looked up at him. He tried to brace himself for whatever Ronald was about to say, and judging from the sympathetic look that passed through Cass's eyes, he was about to get some very shocking news.

"According to my source, Vanessa didn't get involved with another man after you." Ronald paused several snail-crawling moments. "If I were a betting man, I'd say yes, Dominic Cordova has your daughter."

Chapter Three

"Well?" Cass challenged. "Do you finally realize I'm telling the truth?" But she dropped the snarky attitude when Matt groaned, rolled off her and landed on his back on the floor.

"I can't believe this," he said. And he kept repeating it, punctuating it with some profanity.

Cass tried to sit up, but he put his arm across her stomach to keep her down. "I know it's going to take some time to sink in—"

His glare cut her off. "Don't say anything. Don't move," he said, through clenched teeth. "And don't you dare pull out another weapon."

"Because you already have enough to deal with. Yes, I understand that."

Besides, she had no intention of holding him at gunpoint. Not now. That phone call was exactly the impetus that could get Matt Christensen to cooperate with her plan.

Well, maybe.

Maybe he would go in an entirely different direction and try to turn all of this, including her, over to the authorities.

She couldn't let that happen.

Because with Dominic's recent pact with the powers-that-be, no one would be looking hard for evidence to exonerate her. Heck, they might even destroy those surveillance tapes to protect the tenuous relationship they had with a man who could help them catch bigger, meaner fish.

"Truth time," Matt insisted, groaning and turning his head toward her. Unfortunately, that put their faces only a couple of inches apart. Practically eye-to-eye. "Did you doctor that photo?"

"No."

He studied her a moment. "But you had reason to doctor it."

"True, but if I hadn't thought the child was your daughter, I wouldn't have come here." Because all that intimate eye contact was starting to distract her again, she looked away. "I figured...hoped," she said, rethinking, "that you'd want to find Molly."

"How?" he tossed at her like a gauntlet. "Your plan sucks, and it has crater-size holes in it. For instance, if by some miracle you do get inside Dominic's estate, what then? Have you even thought beyond that point?"

"You bet I have. The plan is simple—we find the evidence and your daughter, and we take both her and the surveillance disks and get out of there."

Because he still had his arm slung over her stomach, she felt his muscles tense. "My daughter." A moment later he hissed out a breath. "If it's really true, then why wouldn't Vanessa have told me?"

Cass could think of a reason—maybe the snobbish Vanessa hadn't wanted her middle-class ex-boyfriend to know because she'd had no plans to keep their child—but Cass didn't voice that aloud. Judging from his silence and the way his jaw muscles had declared war on each other, Matt had already drawn the same conclusions.

"Look, I know it'll take you awhile to come to grips with all of this," she said to him. "But the truth is—we don't have time to spare. Remember that part about Dominic recycling disks every year. Well, in eight days it'll be a year since he murdered his business associate and framed me. I have it on good authority that he didn't bother to erase those disks, probably because he's too arrogant to believe he could ever get caught. We have eight days at the most to get the evidence, and each and every one of those days means that your little girl is living under the same roof with a man like Dominic."

His gaze snapped to hers, and his teeth came together. "I don't need that reminder."

She wasn't immune to that emotion she heard in his voice. A father's concern. Even though she wasn't a parent, Cass had no trouble imagining how she would feel if their positions were reversed.

"For what it's worth," she offered, "Dominic's sister, Annette, has apparently been taking care of the child since the adoption. In fact, Annette's the one who wanted a baby, and Dominic adopted Molly for her because she can't have children of her own."

"And that's supposed to make me feel better?"

"It should. Annette's physically handicapped and overly devoted to Dominic, but from everything I've heard about her, she's also, well, human. And kind. I've never met the woman, but I don't believe she'd hurt your daughter."

Cass prayed that was true anyway. Dominic was Annette's baby brother, and Cass figured if it came down to it, Annette would protect Dominic at all cost. Unfortunately, that now involved an innocent baby girl.

She pushed off his arm and got to her feet, not easily. Cass winced at the soreness in her backside and legs. She'd have bruises from their wrestling match, but then Matt likely hadn't escaped injury, either. "You should probably get dressed so we can start making plans to leave."

However, the moment the words left her month, a chill went down her spine. Not because of the leaving part—that was a necessity—but because the full impact of that call hit her. She'd let the news distract her, and it couldn't have come at a worse time.

"Just who was that on the phone anyway?" she asked.

"Ronald McKenzie." Matt got up from the floor. No

wincing for him. He accomplished it quite easily, then put her weapon on the counter next to the tranquilizer gun, picked up his pants and put them on. "He works for the FBI."

That spine chill got significantly worse. "Oh, mercy." She stepped in front of him. "Didn't you hear that part about the leak in official communication's channels?"

"I heard, but I trust Ronald."

"Yes, but you can't trust the people he questioned about your child."

Matt opened his mouth and closed it. Cass could almost see the thought process happening in his head. But what she couldn't determine was where exactly those thoughts were leading.

"You need me to get into Dominic's estate," she said, in case he was thinking about ditching her. "I've been there, and I know the layout. Without me, it'll take you a lifetime or two just to find your daughter."

He just stared at her.

"Okay, maybe not a lifetime," she countered, when that stare crossed over to making her uncomfortable. "But if we do this right, it can be a quick in and out. An extraction, I believe you special agent guys call it. You could bring Molly home where she belongs."

Matt zipped his pants. "Or I could simply ask Dominic Cordova to hand her over to me."

It was an angle Cass had already anticipated, and she had a cautionary answer. "You could, but what happens if he refuses? The Justice Department won't be on your side. You said so yourself. Dominic is their new best friend."

He paused a moment and then shook his head. "You're asking the impossible. I can't break the law. I've sworn—"

"I know." Best to nip the doubt before it could grow into a full-blown argument. "But if we think this through, we may be able to skip anything illegal. For starters, I know the head groundskeeper at the estate. He's a semifriend, and he can hire us as part of the crew who'll be decorating the estate for Christmas. That way we wouldn't technically be breaking and entering."

"No. We'd only be *stealing*. Last time I checked that was still a crime even for former debutantes."

She hated that label and hated even more that it bugged her. And he knew it bugged her.

"You have a right to your daughter," she reminded him. "And Dominic obviously isn't planning on just handing her over, or he would have already done it. If he didn't know beforehand, he certainly suspects now that the adoption was illegal. It was all over the news, and the lawyer who handled Molly's adoption was arrested."

"All of that could mean nothing." But his body language told her that Matt knew she was right.

Cass pushed a little harder. "Here's my suggestion. You ask for some vacation time. If your boss wants to know why, you can say it's some sort of family emergency. Which it is. Then, you *borrow* the jamming equipment, and we can leave immediately. If all goes well, you could be back as soon as the day after tomorrow—with your little girl."

"No," he said, buttoning his shirt.

Stunned, Cass replayed that one word, hoping she'd heard him wrong. "No? To what part of the plan?"

"To all of it."

She replayed that, as well, and it didn't sound any better the fifth time around. "But what about Molly?"

He shrugged. "That's what official channels are for."

Cass could have pointed out all the pitfalls associated with official channels, especially since Dominic was now part of those channels. However, Matt Christensen knew what was at stake here. He knew that Dominic could hide the child so that no one could get to her— ever. He knew what could go wrong, and yet he was obviously willing to risk doing this the *official* way.

"Okay," Cass mumbled. She took a deep breath and pushed her hair away from her forehead. "So, I guess this is goodbye. No hard feelings, I hope."

With that, she started for the door.

She didn't get far.

He snagged her by the arm. "You think you're leaving?"

Since that sounded like a challenge, her chin came up. "I *am* leaving." She tried not to sound hesitant.

But she was. Heaven help her, she was.

Special Agent Matt Christensen had been her best shot at clearing her name. Without him, she didn't stand a snowball's chance in hell of doing that.

"It'd be suicide for you to try to break into Dominic's estate alone," he pointed out.

"I have insider help, remember?"

"Yeah, and if that were enough, you wouldn't have come here in the first place."

Touché.

Yes, she had an insider, Hollis Becker, Dominic's head groundskeeper and the man in charge of external security for the estate. Because she was paying him well, he was good at eavesdropping, keeping track of Dominic and taking the occasional picture for her. But Hollis wouldn't be able to get her past the internal security system there. No, the best he could do was get her a fake job as a seasonal helper, give her a temporary place to stay and tidbits of information as to Dominic's immediate whereabouts. That would give her, perhaps, an opportunity to sneak inside the basement of Dominic's estate.

Cass tried to move out of his grip, but he held on, latching on to her other arm as well. She really hated the idea of kneeing him in the groin, but if it came down to it, she would. If she stayed, she'd end up in jail and therefore, dead.

"Once I'm inside the estate, I'll do everything within my power to get your daughter out of there," she explained, even though it was hard to deliver a calm explanation with her emotions doing a foot race inside her.

He blinked. "You'd actually try to get the baby out?"

"Of course." Cass watched the surprise on his face. No, not just surprise. *Shock.* She frowned. "What, you think I'd leave a child there with Dominic if I had a chance to save her? You must really believe I'm a selfish bimbo."

The hold he had on her melted away, and he groaned and dropped back a step. Cass took it as the gift that it was. She retrieved both of her weapons, and she headed for the back door.

She made it two steps.

"Wait," he said.

Cass stopped. Held her breath. And prayed. Because even though she'd been willing to walk out that door, she knew without his help, she'd fail. Slowly she turned back around to face him.

He opened his mouth to say something. What, she didn't know. And she didn't get a chance to learn because the phone rang again.

Like before, he didn't answer it. He stood there. Waiting. It didn't take long for the answering machine to kick in.

"Matt, it's me, Ronald," the voice said. She recognized it as the man who'd called earlier. Except his voice was a little different now. Not sleepy. Frantic. "I hope to hell you're there listening to this. And I hope to hell I'm wrong."

Matt reached over and hit the speaker function on the phone. "What's going on?" he asked the caller.

"I don't know exactly, but five minutes ago the communications guys at the central command post intercepted a Level Red threat."

Cass looked at Matt, silently requesting an explanation.

He didn't provide one.

"I take it this Level Red has something to do with me?" Matt asked his friend.

"It has everything to do with you. Your name is on it. So is a fugitive—Cassandra Harrison. They believe she's there with you."

That caused Matt to curse.

"What's wrong?" Cass mouthed.

Again he didn't answer.

"My advice is to get out of there fast," Ronald McKenzie continued. "We've got backup on the way, but it doesn't look like we'll make it in time. These guys are five to ten minutes ahead of us."

With that ominous-sounding warning, Ronald McKenzie hung up.

Matt didn't waste any time. He snatched his weapon from the fridge.

"What's wrong?" Cass demanded. "What does Level Red mean?" And she held her breath because she knew she wasn't going to like the answer.

Matt Christensen latched on to her arm and got her moving toward the kitchen door. "It means we leave *now*. Someone sent assassins to kill us."

Chapter Four

"I hate to say I told you so…" Cass grumbled under her breath.

Yeah. Matt hated it, too, but hindsight wasn't going to get them out of this situation.

"Help is on the way, but I doubt they'll arrive in time. And I'd rather not get involved in a shootout," he said more to himself than her.

"Then you'd better have a plan to avoid one."

She added something else equally obvious in that on-the-verge-of-panicking tone, but he shut out whatever she was saying. He had to concentrate if he was going to get them out of this alive.

Matt grabbed the black leather jacket that he kept next to the back kitchen door. He shoved his cell phone, a small supply kit, her tranquilizer gun and some extra magazines of ammo into his pockets. The supply kit had money, matches and just in case, tools for picking locks. While he was at it, he crammed some ammo into

Cass's front jeans pocket, as well. Not the best idea he'd ever had.

His fingers went places they never should have gone.

Cass let him know that with a huff.

Matt mumbled an apology and eased the back door open an inch, but he didn't step outside. He paused and lifted his head a fraction. Listening.

"Won't the assassins use the street out front?" Cass asked. She slid her smaller gun back into her holster.

"Maybe. But they might come at us from several directions."

She sucked in her breath. Yeah. The severity of their situation had obviously sunk in.

Matt opened the door farther and did a situation assessment. He heard the vicious winter wind. But there was no indication that there were assassins about. But then, a hired gun probably wouldn't give many indications before he aimed and pulled the trigger.

Still, they'd have to risk it.

"Let's go," Matt ordered her.

"Let's go?" She didn't move, even when he clamped on to her arm. "How could it possibly be safer out there than it would be in here?"

"Those assassins are going to riddle this house with bullets. There's no place we can hide in here where we can't be shot."

Obviously not convinced, she frantically shook her head. "But—"

"They probably have explosives or some other

heavy artillery they can use to turn this place and our vehicles into fireballs," he interrupted. "We're leaving *now*."

Matt didn't wait for an argument. He pulled her out the door and headed for the first cluster of oaks at the back of the house. It wasn't far, less than twenty feet away. But every step felt like a mile.

By the time he hauled her behind the largest of the trees, his body was already in full adrenaline mode. His gaze whipped from one side of the woods to the other, and he braced his weapon in case he had to fire. But Matt saw no indication that anyone had trespassed—yet.

"Keep your gun ready," he instructed. He pointed toward another cluster of trees just to the east of where they were. "Let's go."

Cass cooperated. Without hesitation or questions she ran, hurdling over a fallen cedar before she ducked into the next barrier of trees.

"Where are we going?" she asked, her breath heavy with every word. Like him, she kept a vigilant watch around them.

He knew the answer, but he didn't think she'd like it. "To a bunker of sorts. We'll wait there until it's safe for us to leave."

"And what will keep the gunmen from finding us there?"

"Nothing."

Her breath got even heavier. "This doesn't sound like much of a plan."

And at the moment it didn't sound like much of a plan to Matt, either. He had an old truck stashed back beyond the bunker, but it'd be a bear to get to it and then get out without drawing attention from the assassins.

Which meant he might have to kill them.

Of course, Matt had known that from the moment he'd first heard about the Level Red threat. Those men had almost certainly come to murder them, and since Matt wasn't ready to die, he was prepared to take them out first.

Matt surveyed the area, then pointed toward a pair of cedar elms with an ankle-deep stream ribboning around them. Just like before, they raced toward cover.

It was winter all right, not that that was news to Matt, but he became brutally aware of just how cold it was when he felt the slushy, partly-frozen water seep right through the leather in his boots.

Matt heard something. The back door to his house. No doubt opened by one of the assassins. The men had probably come in through the front and already searched the place—and now they were ready to look outside. Cass's and his tracks wouldn't be that hard to follow.

Cass must have heard the door, as well, because she dropped to the ground, using the mound of frozen dirt and rocks as cover.

She aimed her gun in the direction of the house. "We don't have time for this," she whispered. "We need to get out of here so we can get that equipment and leave for Dominic's."

So, she did appear to have that mountain of resolve even in the face of assassins. Matt admired that. But that wasn't necessarily a good thing. Because he had a really bad feeling that camaraderie and admiration were not going to be assets where Cass Harrison was concerned. The less he felt about her, good or bad, the better.

He was about to repeat to himself when a flash of movement captured his complete attention.

One of the men, dressed head to toe in black, darted behind an oak. Matt automatically took aim. So did Cass.

It was too little too late.

A bullet came right at them.

FROM THE MOMENT she'd seen those gunmen, Cass had braced herself for the possibility that she'd have to dodge gunfire. What she couldn't have planned for was the deafening blast that sent that bullet their way. The sound ripped through her, spiking her adrenaline and sending her heartbeat racing out of control.

"Stay down," Matt barked.

Just as another bullet slapped into the dirt mere inches from her head.

Cass flattened her body right against the frozen ground, and she tried to find out where the shots were coming from. The angle was all wrong for the bullets to have come from the gunman behind the big tree.

"He's on the roof," Matt informed her, as if reading her mind. He levered himself up and fired.

Cass hadn't braced herself for that, either, and if she'd thought the shooter's rifle was loud, it was a whisper compared to the sonic boom that came from Matt's gun a couple of feet from her ear.

"Did you get him?" she asked, unable to spot the guy who was obviously trying to kill them.

"Not a chance. He's out of range, and he knows it. That's why he's up there."

Oh, mercy. So, they had one shooter out of range and another likely creeping his way through the woods toward them.

"Turn around," Matt ordered her. "And watch our backs."

Cass hadn't thought it could get any worse until he said that. Her heart was no longer just racing, it was banging against her ribs, and she could feel her pulse pound in her ears.

Forcing herself not to panic, she rolled over so that she was on her back. The trees that'd given them so much protection to get to the bunker were now obstacles. Each one could hide a potential killer. Even worse, if she managed to spot him, Cass wasn't even sure she'd be able to shoot. Simply put, her aim had never been tested in a real situation, only at a firing range.

She might die right here, right now. And all because Dominic wanted to make sure she couldn't testify against him.

Those words flashed through her head and fed the adrenaline. They also fed her determination. They had to survive this. They had no other choice. Because if they died, they would never get Matt's child away from Dominic.

Fueled with her new motivation, Cass readjusted her position and her gun so she'd be better ready to fire. And she waited.

Next to her, Matt fired two more shots.

"You said the guy on the roof is out of range," Cass whispered.

"He is. The guy behind the oak moved."

Oh, God. More heart-pounding adrenaline. But Cass stayed focused on her own task. There was no movement in the back of the woods. No sounds, other than those that should be there. So all she could do was wait and pray that Matt was as good a shot as she thought he was.

It didn't take long, mere minutes, for the winter to stake claim to her body. She was bone cold, and her butt had likely frozen. Oh, and her teeth were chattering. *Audibly* chattering. Cass clamped her teeth over her bottom lip and hoped it would help.

Matt fired yet another round and then almost calmly readjusted his arm. "The guy behind the tree is injured. I shot him in the right hand, so he probably won't be shooting at us anymore."

He'd said that so calmly that it took a moment to sink in. Cass hated that she felt nothing but elation over the injury of another human being. But it seemed appropriate, considering this man, this stranger, had been willing to kill them.

"What about the one on the roof?" she asked.

"Still there."

Wonderful. They couldn't get him, but he could certainly do some damage to Matt and her.

There was a cracking noise. A sound that caused both Matt and her to scurry to re-aim. But Cass saw no gunman. Instead, a dead tree limb swooped to the ground.

Matt immediately went back to his original position so he could keep an eye on the roof. "We need to get to that clearing just to your right."

She glanced in that direction, and it was obvious that Matt and she did not share the same definition of a clearing. At best, it was a path. A narrow one. To make matters worse, there weren't nearly enough trees or underbrush, and it'd be easier for the roof shooter to see them and gun them down.

"Why do we need to be there?" she asked.

"I have a truck parked at the end of the clearing."

Cass glanced in that direction. "How far can the roof guy shoot?"

"Five hundred meters, give or take a meter or two."

"My butt and brain are too frozen to do the math. How far do we have to make it down that so-called clearing before we're safe?"

"About halfway."

This time Cass attempted the math, and she figured that was at least thirty running steps. In other words, it was way too far. "And how many bullets can he fire in thirty seconds?" she asked.

He gave her a flat look. "You don't want to know."

Cass groaned softly. "We can't just lie out here. We'll freeze to death. So, what do we do?"

"The clearing," Matt repeated. "First, though, scoop up those dead leaves and twigs around your feet and toss them on top of the makeshift bunker."

It seemed a strange request, but since there was nothing nonstrange about any of this, Cass did as he asked.

Immediately, bullets came hailing down on them.

"Keep moving those leaves," Matt instructed. He returned fire with one hand and did some leaf arranging of his own.

While keeping a grip on her gun and watching their backs, Cass hurried, scooping and tossing, until she'd gathered up everything that was gatherable.

"Now, put your coat up there," Matt added.

Heck, she didn't question that, either, even though once Cass had stripped off the jacket, she went from teeth-chattering to downright freezing. But she didn't forget to remove the picture of Matt's baby. She shoved that into her jeans.

"Take the small black case from my pocket," he continued. "And then help me out of this jacket so you can add it to the leaves."

Cass did that, too, and it required a lot more body touching than she'd anticipated. Specially, touching Matt's chest, abs and arms. It wasn't easy to get a man his size out of a jacket without her practically crawling all over him.

When she'd finished removing his jacket, Cass opened the wallet-size case and found some small tools, cash and a book of matches. "I'm going to set fire to the leaves and coats?" she asked, not believing that was a good idea.

He nodded, then shot at the guy on the roof, ejected the empty magazine and reloaded. "Literally a smoke screen."

Oh. It might work.

But since Cass couldn't come up with anything better, and since the guy was still shooting at them, she used one of the tiny tools to rip off the bottom of her cable-knit sweater to use as kindling. It wasn't easy because of her shaky hands, but she struck the match, and she sheltered the tiny flame until she managed to get the wool-blend fibers to light. She tossed the lit hunk onto the leaves, twigs and coats.

The cold wind actually helped. It fueled her scrawny fire and quickly whipped it into a pile of gray billowing and *suffocating* smoke.

Cass coughed and turned her face from the fire.

Matt didn't turn his face, and he began to peel off his shirt. "There's not enough smoke."

She disagreed but then realized the guy on the roof wouldn't have much trouble seeing down past the smoke and flames. Matt was right. They needed more.

Cass yanked off her sweater and immediately felt the harder sting of the cold. Her white silk camisole wasn't much protection, and it wasn't the best of days to be braless.

Matt tossed his shirt onto one end of the fire; Cass added her sweater to the other end. Both garments caught fire, and both produced a slightly different-colored smoke. It was enough to create a six-foot-high wall that would hopefully conceal them if Matt didn't stand up too straight.

"Let's go," Matt said, and he pulled her to her feet.

Cass didn't even have time to catch her breath before they started running.

Chapter Five

Matt considered every step to be a victory. But of course the only victory that counted was for them to make it through the clearing without getting shot.

He pushed Cass ahead of him so he could shield her as best he could and catch her if she fell. Yet despite the thorny underbrush and the limb-riddled ground, she not only stayed on her feet, she ran even faster than Matt imagined she could. But then, she had a huge motivation to run.

A spray of bullets tore into the ground. They were close, but not close enough. Which told Matt one important thing—the smoke screen had worked. Because if it hadn't, Cass and he would have been dead.

With bullets zinging around them, Matt spotted the crest just ahead. "Hit the ground," Matt ordered. "Slide down."

Cass did. Just as the bullets stopped. She dropped onto her butt and began the descent down the remains of the banks of a ravine. The dark-green rust-eaten truck was there, waiting for them. It didn't look like much, but Matt knew that it worked, and it was their ticket to safety. It was literally his backup, a vehicle he'd placed in the woods in case the worst happened.

"Don't slow down," Matt warned her when they reached the bottom. By now the gunman was probably off the roof so he could come after them.

Cass raced toward the truck, jerked open the passenger-side door and jumped onto the seat. Matt got behind the wheel and used the key that was duct-taped beneath the seat to start the engine. He slammed his foot on the accelerator and got them out of there.

"Stay down," Matt insisted.

She did, sort of. Cass slid lower into the seat, but she kept her attention focused on the side mirror. She also kept a solid grip on her gun. Matt kept watch, as well, and then he got them the hell out of there.

Kicking up ice and dirt, he plowed through the ravine and exited onto a path that would eventually take them to a back road and then the highway.

Matt dodged some scrub oaks, barely scraping past them, and he checked the rearview mirror. No gunman in sight. That didn't mean there soon wouldn't be. He had to make it past the next rise and dry creek bed before he could even start to level his breathing.

Next to him, Cass was doing her own share of heavy breathing. He could see every muscle in her body knotted, the pulse on her neck pounding. The adrenaline was no doubt still pumping through her. It wouldn't last long, and she'd soon have to deal with the inevitable crash.

"I don't see him," Cass announced. "Do you think he'll come after us?"

"Not easily he won't. By now he's probably rushing back to his vehicle. Maybe calling for reinforcements. If we're lucky, he might be making arrangements to get his comrade to the hospital."

Matt knew he should call headquarters. He should report this, especially since he'd discharged his weapon and injured a man. But what if Cass was right? What if there was a breach in security? If so, his personal cell phone would be easy to track.

She checked the mirror again. Then she leaned forward and tried to turn on the heater.

"It doesn't work," he explained, turning off the cold blast of air from the fan. "There's a blanket behind the seat."

While still staying low, she draped her arm over the back of the seat and fished it out. "There's only one blanket?"

He nodded. "Use it. Your lips are turning blue."

Matt wasn't sure she was going to follow his advice, but then she glanced down at the front of her camisole, noticing her very erect nipples. And that wasn't the only thing. The camisole was short, and the shortness revealed several inches of her bare stomach.

He felt that slam of lust shoot through his body, and he silently cursed his brainless reaction.

"Cover up," he snarled.

She did, finally, but she kept her shooting arm free by draping the fake Navajo-design blanket over only half her body. For some stupid reason, she seemed even hotter and more provocative than she did without the blanket.

"All right. I'm covered. Satisfied?" she asked.

Not even close.

Cass glanced at him, sat up in the seat, did a full 360-degree check of their surroundings and, apparently content that they were safe, she opened the glove compartment. "You have a first-aid kit?"

Alarmed, he looked at her. "Are you hurt?"

"No. But you are." She pointed to the jagged slice across his left bicep. He hadn't even been aware of the injury, but it looked to be from a bullet.

She extracted the small travel-size kit and scooted across the seat toward him. Very close to him. She brought with her the scent of the woods. The fragrant cedars. The leaves. The winter soil. The smoke. But she also brought the smell of flowers. Her shampoo, he discovered, when she leaned across him and her hair went right in his face. It was distracting. But not nearly as distracting as having her firm, small breasts pressed against his right arm.

"You saved my life back there," she said, working quickly to clean the wound. "So, while I'm not thrilled about what just happened, I have faith in you."

Matt winced, both at her comment and the poking around she was doing to his injury. "Faith?"

Cass's gaze met his. So did her breath. "Yes. You

know, as in confidence in your ability to keep us alive and get into Dominic's estate."

Matt leaned back to put some distance between them, and he took the ramp that led to Highway 281, which would take them directly into San Antonio. "Don't have that kind of faith in me."

She shrugged and kept working on the bandage. "Too late."

"It's never too late. Let me tell you something about me. I don't play well with others. I do mainly solo assignments because that's the way I like it."

"Keep talking," she insisted. "Because this is going to hurt, and I'd rather you have your mind on something else when I do this—"

Without further warning, she doused his wound with antiseptic. And she was right.

It. Frickin'. Hurt.

Matt barely muffled a groan.

"Besides, faith is sort of a moot point," she continued. "I have to trust you."

Hell. Now they were onto trust. What next? Fuzzy teddy bears and air kisses?

"I'm not the trustworthy type," he ground out while she put some antiseptic cream on the open wound. It stung. Matt could have sworn he saw stars. "I killed a woman once."

With her antiseptic-coated finger poised in midair, Cass stopped. Looked at him again. "Why, because she bandaged your wound?"

He couldn't quite muster up a hollow laugh. "Not exactly. But it might be a valid motive."

"Sorry. But I can't risk you getting an infection." She wiped her hands with some spare gauze. "I need you healed and raring to go."

Need. That word was like *trust* and *faith.* Nails on a proverbial chalkboard. He'd spent his life trying to avoid stuff just like that.

His parents had taught him some valuable lessons, and one of the biggest was that love and personal relationships weren't for everyone, especially him.

"You're freezing," he heard Cass say.

Now she was concerned about his body temperature. When was this going to stop? "I'll live," he growled.

His icy tone and steely glare would have put most people off. It didn't work on her. She sat back down, hip to hip with him, and draped the blanket over both of them. He was about to tell that the closeness just wasn't a good idea, but she spoke first.

"So, where are we going?"

Though it was a valid question, it surprised Matt. After all, he'd just confessed to killing a woman, and he thought that would have piqued her interest and generated a comment or two.

"I still keep a small apartment in San Antonio near my office," he explained. "I need supplies, equipment— including a clean cell phone—and I need to regroup. It shouldn't take us that long to get there this time of night."

"Your apartment is safe?" she asked. There was some concern in her voice this time.

"No. But then, no place is completely safe right now. It does have a good security system, which I actually use since it's in the city, and we can get in and out of there without being seen."

"And what then?"

It was the million-dollar question. Matt was betting she wasn't going to like his answer. "I'll search through department files to see how I can gain access to Dominic's estate. But before I do that, I'll need to make arrangements for you to be sent to a safe house."

Cass was already shaking her head before he finished. "We have to find your daughter and the evidence. It'll go faster if we're working together."

"And it'll put you in even more danger."

More head shaking. "We're talking degrees now. Someone wants to kill us. The danger can't get any worse than that. Besides, we have to work fast. Time isn't on our side."

Matt couldn't argue with her about that, but he could argue about a potential partnership between them. "Remember that part about me not playing well with others?"

"Tough. For this, you have a partner. *Me.*"

So he wasn't going to shake Cass Harrison anytime soon. She was as mule-headed as he was, and he was wasting his breath arguing with her. Besides, if he did stash her away in a safe house, she likely wouldn't stay.

Nope. She'd break out somehow, probably by picking the lock, and that would ultimately put them both in danger because she'd head directly for Dominic's estate alone.

Still, that didn't mean this partnership was going to happen. Matt figured it'd take another run-in with assassins or some other equally life-threatening situation, and then he might be able to talk her into backing off.

Repeating that to himself, he shook his head.

Cass Harrison wouldn't back off if there were a hundred attempts on her life. Still, he'd have to try hard to convince her otherwise.

Because the traffic was heavier, Matt eased his gun into his lap so that it wouldn't be seen by a motorist. He didn't want to have to deal with anyone calling in the local authorities.

The blanket shifted. She moved closer. No longer hip to hip, her left breast was squished against his right arm. With everything else he had going on, Matt just couldn't understand why his body reacted to hers in such a primal way.

"Why did you kill her?" she asked.

He welcomed the question, even though it'd come a little later than he'd anticipated. Still, conversation might help keep his mind off the things it shouldn't be on in the first place. "Having second thoughts about me?"

She made a sound that could have meant anything. "I just want to know why you even brought it up."

Matt frowned. "To show you the kind of man I am."

Cass turned slightly and faced him. The blanket slipped off her shoulder, as did the strap of her camisole. She quickly put them back in place, but not before he got an actual glimpse of the nipple that'd been driving him insane.

"So, what kind of man are you?" she asked. "Was this woman a serial killer or a bank robber—"

"She was innocent," he volunteered. "Never even had a speeding ticket."

When Cass didn't respond, he glanced at her. She was studying him, but that wasn't fear in her eyes. "Then what did she do? Why did she have to die?"

"She loved the wrong man," Matt explained. He turned off the highway and took the street toward his apartment. "During a routine drug bust, things got crazy. The drug dealers fired shots. So did I. This woman jumped in the path of a bullet meant for her crack-dealing boyfriend."

Cass huffed. "That's what I hate about love. It messes with an otherwise rational mind. The woman was an idiot for giving up her life for a worthless piece of slime." She paused, and there was a change in her breathing as if she were uncomfortable with the subject. "Back there, when that man was shooting at our backs, you pushed me in front of you."

It took Matt a moment to switch conversational gears. "So I could catch you if you fell."

"And so I wouldn't be shot. Thank you for that."

He didn't like where this was going. More camaraderie. They didn't need it. "It's what I was trained to do."

"The thank-you still stands. There aren't many people who'd be willing to take a bullet for me. Even if it was your training, it felt good. For the first time in nearly a year, I don't feel alone."

Matt heard her. He even heard her voice crack on the last word. He still wasn't pleased with the conversation, sentimentality or the close contact. But he couldn't give it any more attention than that, because something caught his eye.

A black SUV parked at the end of his street.

"What's the matter?" Cass asked.

"That SUV shouldn't be there." He turned around and drove toward the small park that was two blocks from his apartment. "I don't recognize it."

She looked back. "Maybe one of your neighbors has a visitor or a new car?"

"Not with our luck."

"You're right," she mumbled. "So, does this mean we're not going into your apartment?"

"Oh, we're going in all right." They could follow the park to a greenbelt that would lead them directly to the back steps of the apartment building. "We don't have a choice. There are things we'll need if we want to have any chance of staying alive."

"Just how risky is this?" she asked as he parked behind a huge cedar jungle gym.

"As risky as it gets. You can wait here if you like."

She glanced around before her eyes came back to him. "Not a chance. Let's get this show on the road."

Matt grabbed his gun and opened the truck door. He only hoped he wasn't leading Cass Harrison straight to her death.

Chapter Six

There was a thin greenbelt of trees and shrubs behind Matt's apartment building, and they used the meager cover to get from his truck to the back entrance.

What they didn't do was actually go into the entrance.

Instead Matt stopped about ten yards away. Still hidden in the shrubs, he waited and watched while the bitter cold ate away at them.

Despite her freezing body, Cass understood the hesitation. He was checking for any signs that the assassins were nearby waiting to ambush them. She checked, too, and just when she was certain that hypothermia was about to set in, Matt got them moving again.

With their guns drawn, they made their way into a open corridor and hurried up the stairs. He entered his apartment as if he expected to be ambushed by a team of assassins.

But much to Cass's relief, the place seemed to be empty. Matt didn't turn on the lights, so the only illumination came from the streetlamp and Christmas lights that decorated the windows of the adjacent apartment building. Those multicolored lights threaded through the window blinds.

He double-locked the door behind them and checked the entry closet and the bathroom—the only two places a killer could hide—since it was a one-room studio apartment. It was austere by anyone's standards. There was a tiny kitchen on one side and a living area on the other. The only furniture was a sofa sleeper, armoire and a single bar stool crammed against the kitchen counter.

Matt set the security system and fished through one of the drawers of the armoire. He tossed her a dark-blue shirt.

"Thanks," Cass mumbled, and she quickly made use of it. The apartment was a lot warmer than outside, but it still wasn't exactly toasty.

Matt put on a shirt, as well—a white one. He didn't button it, though. Cass was thankful for the darkness because she knew for a fact it wasn't a good idea to be gawking at his chest.

Except he was gawking at hers.

Cass frowned and glanced down. Her shirt, or rather the shirt he'd loaned her, was unbuttoned, as well, and for some reason that stupid thready light made her white camisole the center of attention.

She buttoned her shirt and lifted her eyebrow.

Matt buttoned his, too.

But that wasn't all he did. He immediately took out a cell phone from the armoire and began to scroll through the numbers.

"There's a leak in communications," she reminded him.

"This phone isn't traceable, and I'll call Ronald McKenzie on his private line."

She couldn't believe what she'd just heard. "Ronald as in the guy you called just before the assassins came after us?"

"Yep. Same guy." And Matt stopped scrolling and pressed the call button.

Cass latched on to his arm. "You can't do this."

"Hey, this is your plan, remember? I'll need jamming equipment to gain entry to Dominic's house."

"Yes, but I thought we'd get the equipment without having to call anyone in the Justice Department."

"Not possible. For starters whoever is trying to kill us will probably be waiting for me outside my office.... Ronald," Matt greeted. Obviously the man had answered his private line. "Tell me what the hell just happened."

Cass couldn't hear what Ronald was saying, so instead she debated if she should try to stop Matt from continuing this call. But she couldn't stop him because they needed that equipment. She only hoped this wouldn't result in another run for their lives.

Matt explained to Ronald what was going on, and then he motioned for her to go to the window. "Keep an eye on that SUV parked outside," he mouthed.

Alarmed that he'd heard something in his conversation about the vehicle, Cass hurried to the window and peeked out the corner of the blinds. The SUV was still there, with the Christmas lights dancing across the darkly tinted windows, but she couldn't see if anyone was inside it.

"So you can get the equipment," she heard Matt say to his fellow agent.

It didn't sound like a question, either. But he did seem conflicted, probably because he was having another battle with his conscience. It didn't stand a chance against the flip side to his dilemma—getting his daughter away from Dominic.

"Okay," Matt continued. "I need another favor. Do a test on the communications channels. See if you can pinpoint that leak." He paused. "Get here as fast as you can. Come in the back way. There's someone in an SUV watching the place."

"He's bringing the equipment?" Cass asked the second he clicked the end call button.

"Hopefully. If there's no hitch."

"Well, maybe we've had our share of hitches already. We're due for a break." She truly believed that. Their luck couldn't be all bad.

"Yeah." For such a simple response, it conveyed a lot of doubts and hesitation. She didn't question Matt's competence as an agent, but this was probably the first time he'd had such a massive distraction.

His daughter.

"Are you coming to terms with fatherhood?" she asked, still keeping her attention on the SUV.

Cass heard the slight shift of his breath. He sank down on the arm of the sofa next to her and checked the magazine in his gun. What he didn't do was answer.

She stared at him a moment, waiting. Studying him. And wondering why he looked so…interesting to her. Yes, he was hot. But there was more. He had that whole bad boy, snarly thing going for him.

Thankfully, she wasn't into snarly bad boys.

She hoped.

"See anything out there?" he asked.

Oh. So, that was the somewhat delayed answer to her question. The subject of fatherhood was off-limits. Not that she hadn't expected it. It might take weeks or even longer for him to get used to the idea.

"I see the SUV," she reported. "There are also three other cars—all empty. And Christmas lights." She thought of Molly. Of how magical the holidays were for a child. Matt's daughter was just old enough to notice the trees and the decorations.

"I miss Christmas," Cass mumbled.

"Yeah," he practically snapped. "I bet holidays at your massive family estate were something else. All that glitter and glitz."

Well, that took care of her nostalgic mood. "No. I miss *Christmas*. Being with friends. Wrapping presents. Baking cookies."

"You bake cookies?" Not quite a snarl, but close.

Cass shifted her position so she could see him but still glance out the window. "There it is again. I took Psychology 101, so I know what's going on here. Transference. Vanessa was a snobby heiress who did a thorough job of stabbing your heart with the heels of her overpriced designer stilettos. So, you assume that I, too, am a snobbish heiress capable of only thinking of myself. And maybe I was, once. But look at me—I don't look so rich and snobby now, do I?"

Much to her surprise, he did look at her. *Really* looked at her with those intense Nordic-blue eyes. "I have no idea why I want to kiss you."

She sputtered out a cough of surprise. And mentally scrambled to come up with an explanation. Thankfully, one came that didn't involve *her* attraction to bad boys. "Psych 101 again—you want the distraction so you won't have to deal with the thoughts of fatherhood. Danger you can handle. In fact, you thrive on it. But fatherhood, that scares you, doesn't it?"

The snarl returned. It was coupled with a low growl in his throat. And a lethal glare. She'd crossed the line. Cass swallowed hard and would have moved away from him.

There wasn't time.

He reached out. Lightning fast. Because he was still holding his gun, both his hand and his Glock went around the back of her neck. She felt the cold steel on her skin.

And she felt him, hot and bad.

Matt dragged her closer. Snapped to him. His mouth went to hers.

And he kissed her until she went limp.

THE KISS WASN'T SLOW and lingering.

It was hard and punishing.

Definitely not a kiss of foreplay or romance. Okay, maybe there was some passion, but it ended so quickly that Matt didn't have time to think.

He didn't want to think.

All he knew was that he didn't dare allow the kiss go on. Not with her seemingly willing mouth. So, he let go of Cass and ran his tongue over his bottom lip. "I was right. Even in those clothes and with that bad haircut, you taste expensive."

"You taste dangerous," she countered.

The corner of his mouth hitched. Not a smile. Not a smile of humor, anyway. It was the smile of a man who knew exactly what all of this meant. Cass no doubt knew, too.

She *was* expensive.

He *was* dangerous.

They were opposites, and they were attracted to each other.

But the truth was that attraction was all hormones and the need for a diversion. That smile also hopefully told her that they wouldn't be doing it again anytime soon.

Even if his body clamored that it would like to go another round.

"Say it," he grumbled. It was time to put some new barriers between them. "I'm a jackass."

"You're a jackass," Cass accommodated. "But—"

"No more Psych 101 babble. I'm a jackass Justice Department agent. You're an expensive-tasting fugitive. If we're lucky, we'll get into Dominic's place, take my daughter and find the evidence you need. Then we'll part company and never see each other again."

"Absolutely." And she sounded downright perky about it, too.

Well, what the heck had he expected? They both had personal stakes in this, but those stakes were at opposite ends of the proverbial spectrum. Despite her claims to the contrary, if it came down to it, Cass would do what it took to save *herself.* And he would do what it took to rescue his daughter. They weren't partners.

More like two surly prison escapees handcuffed together.

Who'd just kissed.

"Say something," he insisted.

She stared at him. "Say something, but not about that kiss, right?"

"Damn right."

"Okay. Let's talk about Dominic's sister, Annette." There was no perkiness in her voice now, and she had her attention back on the SUV. "I never met her. She was away in Europe during the short time that Dominic and I were together. But I've been doing a lot of research about her. She's not like Dominic, and I'm sure she loves Molly."

Okay, that was a good subject. "Does Annette love Molly enough to just hand her over to her real father?"

"You mean if you contact her, will she willingly relinquish custody to you?" She lifted her shoulder and paused, her forehead bunched up. "Maybe."

The answer surprised him more than a little. He'd expected Cass to take the stance that she and only she could help him rescue his daughter.

"But Dominic might not let Annette give up Molly," Matt continued.

Cass shrugged again. "Dominic is…territorial. And manipulative. If he learns that Molly's father is a federal agent, he'll likely try to use her to get whatever he wants from you and the Justice Department."

Matt had already come to that conclusion. He only hoped that Dominic wouldn't make that connection before they could get on the estate.

"You'll get your daughter," she said. "Because you're good at what you do. Because you don't fail."

"I've been failing most of my life," he heard himself say. And he groaned. Hell's frickin' bells. What was it about this woman that made him want to kiss her and then pour out his heart?

"You failed at something?" She used the same tone he'd used for his smart-mouth, baking-cookies remark. A tone that set his teeth on edge.

So, he told her the truth.

"Yeah. I failed. I grew up in a run-down apartment with a neo-hippy single mom who didn't believe in steady employment or parenting. When I was eight, she was murdered by a homeless lunatic who thought she was trying to steal his shopping cart filled with trash. Because no relative would take me, I was sent to foster care and screwed up my life in just about every way possible."

"You couldn't have screwed up that much. After all, you're a federal agent."

"Juvenile records are sealed," he pointed out. Because he needed something to do, he switched places with her and kept watch on the SUV. "I also had a mentor, someone who cared enough to make sure that I not only qualified for the agency, but that I succeeded."

And that mentor was none other than his present boss, Gideon Tate.

"So you got a second chance," Cass said as a matter of fact. "That's what I want. A chance to prove I'm innocent so I can go home and run the family business that I inherited two years ago when my parents were killed. No more bimbo labels for me. And no more men." She paused. "No more kisses, either."

"Agreed," he said quickly.

"I'm not a multitasking sort of person," Cass admitted. "And right now the only thing I can concentrate on is getting into Dominic's estate."

Matt was about to agree, but movement in the

parking lot caught his eye. The passenger door of the SUV opened. He automatically lifted his weapon and braced himself for another attack.

"What's wrong?" Cass hurried to the window and peeked out the other side of the blinds.

Matt watched as the tall, athletically-built brunette exited the SUV. And he cursed under his breath.

"You know her?" Cass asked.

"Yes. That's Libby Rayburn, a fellow agent." She was dressed all in black and was clutching a small handheld device. Matt was betting it wasn't a Black-Berry. It was probably an infrared thermal scanner.

"What's she doing here?" Cass wanted to know.

Matt could think of a reason—but it wasn't a good one. She would obviously have known about the Level Red threat and was there to check on him.

His phone rang, and he checked the caller ID and saw Libby's name there. "Matt," he answered.

"Thank God you're all right."

Libby sounded genuine enough. Matt hoped she was. He'd worked side by side with her for two years and trusted her. Well, at least, he had before tonight.

There weren't many people he trusted now.

"I know you're in your apartment," Libby informed him. "I scanned it with infrared. Don't worry. I've been monitoring signals, and no one else has attempted to scan the place."

That was good. But it didn't mean it would stay that way.

"Who's with you?" Libby asked.

"It's a long story. I'm more concerned about a leak in the department communications and the fact that someone tried to murder me."

Libby didn't answer right away. "We're looking into that. For now I have the parking lot fully monitored."

"Well, it can't be that secure because I got in," Matt pointed out.

"Through the greenbelt. Yes. I missed that at first, but it's covered now."

Matt didn't know what to make of that. "Considering there's almost certainly a leak in communications, I'm not relieved about that. The person responsible for that leak could already be here."

"I'm monitoring the area with equipment, not agents." She glanced down at the screen of the infrared device. "I'm coming up."

And that's exactly what she proceeded to do.

"It's late," Matt said. "I'm with someone." He caught on to Cass and pulled her closer to him. She gave him a puzzling glance and even a nudge in the ribs with her elbow. "Play along," he mouthed. "She's monitoring us with infrared."

Cass quit struggling and stared at Matt.

Because he figured there was nothing he could say to stop Libby from walking up the stairs, he had a decision to make. If he didn't answer the door, she'd probably knock. That might alert neighbors. It might also make Libby more concerned than she apparently already was. Heck, maybe she thought he was being held hostage or something. Either way, he didn't want her there. She'd have too many questions, and besides, Ronald was on the way with the equipment. Matt definitely didn't want to have to answer anything about *that*.

Matt clicked the end call button, caught on to Cass's arm and pulled her toward the door. "Keep your weapon out of sight," he instructed.

"Are you going to tell me what's going on?" Cass asked.

There was a soft knock at the door. "Keep your face hidden, and pretend you're my lover."

Cass's mouth dropped open. "Huh?"

He didn't really have time for a further explanation, but Cass caught on, anyway. If Libby thought they were on the verge of having hot sex, she might leave right away.

Cass stuffed her gun into the back slide holster of her jeans, and Matt waited until she stepped behind him before he opened the door to face his fellow agent.

Not that she looked much like an agent.

Libby looked more like a model. Tall, attractive. She also had a brooding intensity and was married to the badge. In the two years that Matt had known her, she'd never spoken of her personal life. It was one of the reasons Matt enjoyed working with her. There was nothing wrong with being all business.

Except he no longer felt that way.

Molly had changed the way he felt about a lot of things.

Libby's curious blue eyes landed on him first. Then, what she could see of Cass's arm.

"Libby, I'm with a friend," Matt offered. And that was the only introduction he intended to make.

"You don't want me here," Libby said. "Yes, I got that from your tone. But you need help, Matt. Were you hurt in the attack?"

"Not a scratch," he lied. Matt didn't want to answer questions about that, either.

Libby's mouth tightened. "Do you really think I believe you're about to haul this woman off to bed?"

"Adrenaline lust." Matt dragged Cass even closer. She did her part. Cass snuggled close to his back while keeping her face hidden.

Libby made a sound to indicate she didn't believe any of this. "Are you planning to stay here tonight?"

"Yes," Matt lied again.

He didn't have to add to the lie, either, because Cass's phone buzzed softly. She grabbed it from her pocket and glanced at the screen. "I need to take this call," she whispered. She headed for the bathroom and even shut the door.

That grabbed Matt's interest. Who would be calling Cass, and was it related to Dominic and his daughter?

But Matt didn't have time to ponder that.

"This could be trouble," Libby announced, looking at the infrared screen. "A car just stopped at the far end of the parking lot."

Matt pulled her inside, kicked the door shut and went to the window. His body automatically went into combat mode. Until he spotted the car and the person inside.

It was Ronald.

Matt turned to Libby. "Do you trust me?"

She blinked. "Of course."

"Then leave now."

"I can't. Someone tried to kill you tonight."

"And there's nothing you can do about that here. What would help is for you to go back to headquarters and find out about that leak."

Matt didn't wait for her to agree. He caught on to her and practically dragged her toward the door. Just as his phone vibrated. It was Ronald, no doubt, calling to see if it was safe to come up.

"I'll contact you soon," Matt promised Libby. He pushed her out the door and locked it. Matt waited until he heard her walk away before he answered the call.

"Libby is here at the apartment building," Matt immediately told Ronald. "She should be on her way to her SUV now. Do you see her?"

"Yes. What'd she want?"

"To check on me. She knows nothing about the equipment. I want to keep it that way."

"So do I," Ronald agreed. "If anyone in the department learns why I really checked out this stuff, then both of us will be in hot water."

Definitely. "I take it that you got what I need?" Matt asked.

"I got it. I signed it out of the equipment room with an explanation that I planned to use it to assist in tracking the assassins who came after you."

"Good thinking." Matt watched through the window as Libby got in her vehicle and drove away. "Duck down in the seat. Libby's about to drive by, and even though she's using an infrared scanner, I'd rather she not see your face."

"You and me both," Ronald mumbled.

Matt waited, dividing his attention between Libby's exit and the muffled phone conversation that Cass was having in the bathroom. He couldn't hear enough of what she was saying to know if this was good or bad news.

"Libby's gone," Matt relayed to Ronald.

Ronald didn't waste any time. He drove closer, got out and hurried toward the apartment. Matt had the door open and ready for him.

Unlike Libby, this particular co-worker was a welcome sight, because Ronald wasn't just a co-worker, he was as close to a friend as Matt had. He was wiry with black hair that lay flat and slick, and eyes that were too big for his face. The only thing that saved him from looking downright spooky was his easy smile.

"Here's the infrared monitor, a jammer, laptop and binoculars with a long-range viewer," Ronald explained, handing Matt a bulging leather equipment bag.

Matt lifted a pair of handcuffs from the bag. "You're optimistic—I don't think I'll be able to make an arrest this time around. Nor will I have time for kinky sex."

Though he would no doubt be thinking about kinky sex with Cass around.

Ronald shrugged. "They came standard issue with the bag. Ditto for the stun gun and plenty of other stuff. What's missing is the thermal body armor device. It wasn't there. Guess somebody screwed up and forgot to include it."

Matt didn't mind not having the thermal body armor. It was a tiny device, and it basically blocked an agent from being detected with an infrared monitor. But since Matt was the one who'd be using the monitor on Dominic and his guards, he likely wouldn't need it.

"I don't suppose it'd do me any good to try to talk you out of whatever it is you're about to do?" Ronald asked.

"No good whatsoever." Matt turned on the infrared to test it. It worked. He could see Cass's "hot" image in the bathroom.

"This is about the baby that Dominic adopted," Ronald continued. He cocked his head to the side. "Yours and Vanessa's baby."

Because Ronald had risked a lot by coming here, Matt felt he owed him an explanation, even if it was a partial one. "I have to get my daughter out. And please save your breath about going through official channels."

"Wouldn't dream of it." There was more than a touch of sarcasm in Ronald's voice. "Nor will I dwell on the fact that this could cost you everything."

Matt met his gaze head-on. "My daughter is everything now."

Ronald flashed one of his infamous smiles. "I wouldn't respect you if you'd said otherwise." The smile was short-lived. "Gideon is already suspicious. He called me on the way over here."

Their boss. Gideon Tate. And, yeah, Gideon would be suspicious. He was no dummy. Gideon would probably be on Matt's side in this issue, too, if he learned the whole story, but Matt didn't want to drag him into this. The fewer people who knew, the better. That might prevent Dominic from learning what Matt planned to do.

"If you're going to Dominic's estate," Ronald continued, "and if you get in a tight spot, there's a local sheriff nearby that you can trust. Only one. His name is Mike Medina, and he's over in a little town called Rim Rock."

"The department knows this guy is clean and not working for Dominic?"

Ronald nodded. "He's a straight arrow." He glanced around. "What about transportation—how do you plan to get to West Texas?"

"I came here in the truck," Matt volunteered.

Ronald groaned, extracted his keys from his pocket and shoved them into the equipment bag. "You won't get far in that truck. Take my car—the plates are clean. I switched them before I came over. Do you need me to go with you?"

"No. You've already risked enough."

And speaking of risks, the infrared monitor detected some motion. A vehicle moving in the parking lot. Matt went to the window, looked out and saw Libby. She parked, got out and was headed straight for the apartment.

"Libby," Matt relayed to Ronald. "You need to leave so she doesn't see you."

"I have a better idea." Ronald returned to the door. "Since I no longer have the equipment on me, I'll run interference for you and talk Libby into going home. Good luck finding your daughter."

Matt thanked him, locked the door again and hoped like the devil that he wouldn't have to go another round with Libby or the assassins tonight. But he did have to find out what was going on with Cass. She'd been on that phone a long time.

She opened the bathroom door the moment he reached for the knob. "You have the equipment?" Cass asked, glancing at the large black leather bag.

Matt nodded and was about to ask about the call, but the knock at the door stopped him.

"It's Libby," she called out. "I don't care what Ronald says, I can help you."

"We don't have time for another conversation," Cass informed him.

Matt agreed. He opened the bathroom window and tossed out the chain fire escape ladder. It was well past time they got out of there, and leaving the back way was not only safe, it would prevent another encounter with Libby.

"That call was from Hollis Becker, my insider at Dominic's estate," Cass continued. "There's a problem."

He cursed, not just with Cass's news, but the fact that Libby was still pounding his door.

Matt slipped the equipment bag over his shoulder so he could climb down. "What's wrong?" he asked, dreading what he was about to hear.

"Hollis overheard Dominic's sister, Annette, talking to someone on the phone."

Matt's heart dropped to his knees. "Did something happen to Molly?"

"Not like you think. But according to what Hollis overheard, Annette is worried about Dominic. He's involved in some kind of new deal, and she's afraid it might put them all in danger. Annette is making plans to take Molly out of the country."

He mentally filled in the blanks. If Annette managed to get out of the country with Molly, then Matt might never find his daughter. But if Annette and Molly stayed, their lives were at risk.

Matt didn't care for either scenario.

"Let's go," Matt ordered. "We're leaving for Dominic's estate. *Now.*"

Chapter Seven

Four hundred and seventy-three miles.

That was the distance between Matt's apartment in San Antonio and Dominic's isolated Texas estate that was practically on the border with New Mexico. Cass knew the exact mileage because Matt and she had taken turns driving through the night to get there. But they'd finally arrived after a few stops for gasoline, clothes and fast food.

Cass checked her watch. It was 9:00 a.m. Cold, gray and drizzling. It was hardly the hour or the ideal weather to attempt a break-in.

Still, they might not have a choice.

If Annette was leaving with Molly, they'd have to stop her.

When the estate came into view, Matt slowed the car to a crawl on the narrow two-lane private road. Centered among acres of fenced flat land, it was the second time Cass had seen the place. Not a home, exactly. More like a fortress.

Or the gateway to hell.

The three-story Romanesque-style house was constructed of rough-faced squared gray stones that blended into the wintry landscape and gunmetal skies.

Matt and she, however, wouldn't blend.

"Too bad we don't have one of those cloaks like Harry Potter," she mumbled. She took out her phone and pressed in the number for her contact, Hollis Becker. "Then we could make ourselves invisible and walk right onto the grounds and into the house."

Matt eased over onto the shoulder of the road and pointed to the trio of semis that were parked just inside the black wrought iron entry gates. He took some binoculars from his equipment bag and looked around.

"They're putting up Christmas decorations," he relayed to her.

"That's for Dominic's big Christmas Eve party. Thankfully, there'll be so many temporary workers and guests, we won't be noticed."

She hoped.

"Hollis," Cass greeted when the man answered the phone. "It's me. We made it. How soon can you get us onto the estate?"

"Now. Drive through the service entrance. I'll meet you there and tell the guards that you're part of today's work crew. Keep your guns out of sight."

"Will do." She tucked her gun in her back waist holster and stuffed the equipment bag under the seat. "Go straight ahead, then turn right at the service entrance."

Matt proceeded to do just that, and he slipped his own gun inside the brown bomber-style jacket they'd bought at a 24/7 discount store. Cass had gotten stuck with a blue wool coat that was at least two sizes too big, but it'd been the first one she'd grabbed off the rack.

"How much do you trust Becker?" Matt asked.

"Enough. I've paid him well."

He groaned softly and cursed, indicating that he didn't approve of this arrangement. Neither did she, but that didn't mean she wouldn't use Hollis's assistance to get them onto the estate.

"Correction—I've paid him *very* well. To the tune of a quarter of million dollars," she added.

Matt's left eyebrow rose. "How did you get your hands on that kind of money? Your assets are frozen."

"The feds missed a safety deposit box that contained most of the family jewels. No pun intended. I sold or pawned nearly everything inside it."

His eyebrow stayed high.

"We knew this would be risky coming in," Cass said in defense of her plan. "Hollis might be in this for the money, but that doesn't mean he'll betray us. If you ask me, we've got more to worry about from your fellow co-agents, Libby and Rodney, than we do from Hollis."

"Rodney helped us by getting us this car and the equipment. And in all the time I've worked with both of them, I haven't seen anything to indicate they're criminals."

"But we don't know for sure what their motives are.

Either of them could have been responsible for that leak in communications. Either of them could be on Dominic's payroll."

Judging from the throaty grunt Matt tossed her way, he wanted to argue that, but he couldn't. They approached the gate of the service entrance, where four armed guards were waiting for them.

"They're carrying AK-47s," Matt relayed to her in a mumble. "These aren't amateurs."

No. And there wouldn't be amateurs inside the estate, either. As she'd already briefed Matt, Dominic had approximately a dozen guards on duty at all times, and every inch of the house was wired for surveillance.

Just ahead, she spotted Hollis, the wind slapping against his combed over flame-red head of hair. He said something to one of the guards, and the man waved them through the security gate. Hollis pulled his hand from his thick parka so he could open the back door and climb in on the seat behind Cass.

"Take a left up there," Hollis said.

His austere, almost gruffly barked order caused Matt to eyeball the man in his rearview mirror. "This had better not be a trap," Matt warned.

"As long as I get paid, no traps."

Matt glared at Hollis before exchanging glances with her. Obviously, Hollis's comment did nothing to ease the distrust in Matt's eyes.

They used a road that ran along the perimeter of the estate and stopped at a trio of small gray stone cottages. "Stay in the one on the right," Hollis informed them.

"And the other two?" Matt asked.

"Empty this time of year." Hollis got out and started walking back toward the main house. Matt parked the car behind the cottage, so that it wouldn't be in the direct line of sight of the main house. After he made sure that Hollis was indeed leaving, he grabbed the equipment bag, and they went inside.

"Home sweet home," Cass mumbled.

It wasn't the Ritz. Not that she'd expected it to be since these sleeping quarters were obviously for Dominic's workers. Gray linoleum floors ruptured with thin cracks. A rust-scabbed fridge. A hotplate crusted with heaven knows what. A radio so old that it could be considered vintage. A closet-size bathroom that'd seen much better days.

And a bed.

Just one.

A twin size at that.

Either Matt or she was going to end up sleeping on that cold linoleum floor.

But Matt didn't pay any attention to the decor or sleeping arrangements. He also didn't waste any time. He took a handheld device from the equipment bag and turned it on. He angled the device in all corners of the cottage, studied the screen and then went to her.

And that wasn't all.

He put his mouth right against her ear.

"No listening devices," he whispered. His breath was warm, and it sent a shiver of heat through her.

Cass quickly pushed that away and made sure she kept at least a few inches between them when she asked, "Then why are you whispering?"

Once more, he closed the gap between them. His mouth went to her ear again. "There could be some long-range external monitors to detect the sound waves bouncing off the glass."

Oh. Well, this wasn't going to be fun. One bed and they'd practically have to touch to speak, but at least they were on the estate and closer to getting what they both wanted.

Matt turned on the radio, setting it on low volume. It was a country music station, and Keith Urban began to serenade them. "It'll diffuse the sound waves if anyone is trying to listen," he whispered.

Matt then got to work setting up yet more equipment he took from the bag. One piece she recognized as an infrared monitor. Just as he'd done with the "bug" detector, he aimed it in all directions before pointing it at the house.

"There's no one in the immediate area around us," he explained in a whisper. "But there are lots of people inside the estate."

Cass moved closer so she could see the splotches of colors. Matt was methodical, slowly moving the monitor so he could study each room.

And then he stopped.

Cass knew why. One of those people splotches was much smaller than the rest. He stared at it for several moments and then reached for his long-range binoculars.

"Binoculars can't see through walls," she mumbled.

"But they can see through glass," he countered. Matt kneeled down on the floor and aimed the binoculars to the east side of the estate. "I think Molly's in the garden room with three other—"

He froze again.

Alarmed, Cass tried to see what had rendered him speechless and visibly shaken. "Please don't tell me something is wrong."

Still not saying anything, Matt passed the binoculars to her. Dreading what she might see, Cass looked through them and saw what had no doubt alarmed him.

She spotted the guard first. He was by the exterior doors. But then she saw Molly, sitting in a stroller in the lush plant-filled garden room. The little girl looked precious, dressed in pink overalls and a white eyelet lace top.

Annette was there, too, in her wheelchair. Looking rather upset. She had a death grip on one handle of Molly's stroller.

So, did Dominic. He was gripping just as tightly to the other handle.

Cass didn't have to hear them to know that Annette and Dominic were in the throes of a fierce argument.

And Molly was literally right in the middle.

MATT WAITED A MOMENT, until he could hammer down some of the rage that was churning inside him. Mixed with all that rage were fatherly emotions brought on by seeing his daughter for the first time. And Matt had no doubt that this child was his. He could feel it in every part of his soul.

"Are you okay?" Cass whispered.

Matt didn't even try to lie. "No."

He was a powder keg of raw nerves, and that wasn't good. Because that meant he wasn't focused on the mission, and this mission was too damn important for him not to concentrate on what had to be done.

"Call Hollis," Matt said under his breath. He snatched the binoculars from her. "Ask him the best way to approach the house."

Thankfully, Cass didn't remind him that they couldn't go in during broad daylight. She simply made the call, while Matt watched the scene unfold in front of him.

Dominic and Annette were still arguing, or at least having a spirited discussion, but Molly was asleep and therefore oblivious to what was going on around her. Thank God.

She was so little.

So helpless.

Matt studied that tiny face and saw pieces of himself. The way her eyes were set. Her mouth, that was his, too. As was her coloring. Part of him was furious that Vanessa hadn't told him about their baby, and the other part of him just wanted to run into the house and get her out of there.

How would Molly react to him?

He'd be a stranger, of course, but Matt intended to do something about that. He wasn't sure of the logistics yet, but he would be a major part of his daughter's life. He'd be a father in every sense of the word, but it made him a little squeamish to think of holding that tiny girl in his rough hands.

Behind him, he could hear Cass's softly spoken conversation. He could also hear the disappointment in her voice. So it was no surprise when she ended the call and gave him a summary of what Hollis had told her.

"He says it's too risky to go in now," Cass mouthed.

Yeah. Matt knew that.

She moved closer to him, leaned down and whispered the rest in his ear. "It's a long shot, but Hollis says he'll check and see if he can *coax* one of the guards into leaving his post. If he can, he'll give us a call."

Her breath was warm. Mint-scented. She smelled soft and feminine.

Matt kept watch on the garden room. "Hollis means he'll *coax* the guard for a price," he mumbled.

And Cass's silence indicated he was dead on.

Matt made a mental note to repay Cass for all of this.

She stared at him. "Are you thinking about storming the place?" she mouthed.

Matt had dodged her similar questions on the drive

over—mainly because he was still trying to work out everything. But he hadn't ruled out extreme measures.

"What would you do if I said yes?"

Cass shrugged. "Gather the gear, check my weapon." She put her palms together. "Pray. Maybe whine just a little."

A smile tugged at his mouth. Why, he didn't know. There was nothing humorous about this. But it did seem strange that the one person he could trust most in all of this was Cass. In fact, with that possible leak in communication at the Justice Department, she might be the *only* one he could trust.

That was a sobering thought.

"We're screwed if Hollis betrays us," he mumbled.

Cass made a sound to indicate that was true, and she sank down on the floor next to him. Right next to him, so that her arm was against his body. "What's going on in the garden room?"

Matt watched for the latest. "The argument seems to be winding down," he whispered. "And Dominic seems to be winning."

"Not exactly a surprise."

No, it wasn't. From what he knew about him, Dominic would win this argument and all others with his sister. Matt had to get his baby out of there fast, especially since this new business deal that Hollis had learned about could mean extra danger for Molly.

Dominic walked away from his sister and Molly. The image was so clear that Matt could see Annette catch her bottom lip between her teeth and wipe tears from her cheeks. The woman waited there a moment before she got her wheelchair moving, and pushed the stroller out of the garden room.

And out of view.

Whatever that argument had been about, it'd obviously upset Annette.

Matt grabbed the thermal infrared monitor and scanned the house so that he could keep track of Molly. Cass adjusted her position, getting even closer, and she watched the screen, as well. The thermal images were blurry, but Matt guessed that Annette took the baby into the nursery. It was practically in the center of the house, which meant it had no exterior windows or doors.

No easy access.

Still, the nursery was probably their best bet to orchestrate an extraction since it was likely the only time his daughter would be alone.

"That's Dominic," Cass whispered eagerly tapping the screen. "Well, that's his office, anyway. He doesn't let many people in there so that must be him."

Matt hoped that was true because that room was far away from the nursery.

"Look." Cass pointed to the nursery area on the screen. "I think Annette's rocking Molly."

Judging from the motion, it was probably true. That caused Matt a little more concern. It was midmorning, so what was his daughter doing napping? Was she ill?

Hell.

Just that thought sent another slam of adrenaline through him. He had to stop this. Neither his body nor his brain could handle the emotional roller coaster.

"You think Molly's sick because she's asleep?" he asked.

Cass shook her head. "Babies take naps all the time. I'm sure she's fine. Hang in there. We're going to get her out, maybe as soon as today if Hollis can find a coaxable guard."

It wasn't the first time she'd made a promise like that to him. A promise she couldn't keep. But Matt appreciated the gesture.

Heck, he appreciated *her.*

And it didn't have anything to do with this crazy attraction and physical closeness between them.

Did it?

Man, he hoped not. He hoped that his testosterone levels didn't influence something as important as his concentration at a time like this.

A new song came on the radio. Johnny Cash singing "Flesh and Blood." A song of need and lust, or love, depending on the listener's interpretation. Matt didn't have to think hard to know what his interpretation was.

"Uh-oh." She blinked. "You look as if you have something on your mind."

He did—he wanted to kiss her again. Apparently, he hadn't learned a thing from their last kissing episode.

Neither had Cass.

She put her arms around him and pulled her to him.

For comfort, no doubt. For a good reason. He probably looked as torn as he felt.

And that's perhaps why Cass did the unthinkable. *She* kissed *him*.

It wasn't tentative, either. Cass leaned in and pressed her mouth to his. It was a gentle kiss of reassurance. And it probably would have stayed that way if Matt hadn't upped the ante.

He pulled her to him and deepened the kiss. Why? Because he was an idiot and totally incapable of resisting a woman he should be doing everything to resist. But there wasn't a thread of resistance on his part.

Matt dragged her even closer, so that their bodies met, her breasts against his chest. Still, she didn't pull away. She stayed there holding him. Allowing him to kiss her until he no longer felt as if the world was closing in around him.

Gasping for air, she pulled away and ran her tongue over her bottom lip. "You still taste dangerous."

That was actually a relief. Because he didn't want that kiss to be anything more than it was—a reaction to the emotional hell they were going through.

"You still taste expensive," he countered.

She smiled. "Then we're safe."

And unfortunately he knew exactly what she meant.

His phone buzzed. He'd set it that way because he thought a ring might be overheard. "Saved by the buzz," he mumbled. Heaven knows he needed something to slap him back to reality.

But after glancing at the caller ID, he wasn't so sure this was the slap he needed.

"It's Libby," he relayed to Cass.

The call shouldn't have made Matt feel so blasted uncomfortable, but it did. Probably because Cass had put it in his head that neither Ronald nor Libby could be trusted.

"Is this line secure?" Matt immediately asked Libby when he answered the call.

"Yes. I'm actually using my home phone. I didn't think it'd be wise to talk to you while I was at the office. Especially with what I have to tell you. Matt, there's a problem with some of the files related to Dominic."

"What do you mean?" He remembered to keep his voice low just in case.

"Information is missing. Heck, entire files are missing. I've been digging, and I don't like what I've found in the ones I have managed to access. It's about Cassandra Harrison."

Well, Matt certainly hadn't expected her name to come up in this conversation. He moved closer to Cass and put the phone in between them. "What about Ms. Harrison?" Matt prompted Libby.

"I think there's someone in the department who doesn't want any evidence found that could exonerate her."

Beside him, he felt Cass tense. He tensed, too. "You have proof?"

"More like a theory. You already know about the deal the department made with Dominic. He'll give them information about his criminal buddies so he can get immunity for himself. Well, it's possible Dominic got something else out of that deal—an agreement that Cass Harrison's name wouldn't be cleared because it would ultimately cast suspicion of murder on him."

That certainly meshed with what Cass had been saying. Which brought Matt to something he'd realized in the past twelve hours. Cass wasn't guilty.

"I'd like to know who orchestrated this deal with Dominic," Matt insisted.

"So would I, but those are the missing files. I've talked to Ronald, and he thinks I'm jumping the gun, that there is no conspiracy to frame Ms. Harrison."

But Matt believed that was exactly what was happening. Ronald would, too, once he looked at all the facts.

Hopefully.

"Name names," Matt said to Libby. "Who do you think is behind this?"

Libby didn't say anything for several seconds. "I hate to say it, but maybe Ronald. He could be the one tapping into official communications, too. There aren't many people in the department who could manage that. He has the expertise for it."

Matt frowned. "So do you."

"Yes. But I didn't. And neither did you. Unless you're willing to consider Ronald, that leaves us where we started."

Not quite.

"Thanks for the info, Libby. I'll be in touch." Matt clicked the end call button and turned to Cass.

Oh, she knew where this was leading. He could see it in her eyes. "Right after we *met,* you said you'd phoned in some bogus information to someone you thought you could trust in the Justice Department," Matt reminded her. "After the person had the bogus info, it was relayed to Dominic. Through a secure line at his estate, you said. I'm guessing that Hollis tapped Dominic's line for you."

She nodded.

"But what you haven't told me is the name of the person you thought you could trust in the Justice Department."

Cass took a moment to answer. "Your boss, Gideon Tate. He was a friend of my father's. I've known him for years."

This was the first Matt had heard about Gideon knowing Cass. And he didn't like it. Cass's name had come up several times in conversation between Gideon and him, so why hadn't his boss mentioned it?

"Why didn't you have Gideon get the equipment for you?" Matt asked.

She took another moment. "He was first on my list, until I verified that leak."

"But Gideon wasn't necessarily responsible for that."

"No. But I couldn't risk it. Besides, you had the best motive for coming here."

True. Yet Matt couldn't help but wonder just how much Gideon knew. There was only one way to find out. He pressed in the numbers to what was supposed to be Gideon's secure line.

"Not a good idea," Cass said catching on to his arm. "Gideon can track your cell phone."

"Not this phone." It was secure, as Gideon's line was supposed to be. Which obviously wasn't very comforting. But Matt needed to do his own test. "Gideon," he said when his boss answered. "It's Matt. I need to give you a situation report about the assault."

"Where are you?" Gideon immediately asked.

"At a friend's house. I was hurt in the attack. Not badly, but I need to lay low for a few days."

"I want you to come here. Or better yet, I'll come and get you. I'll bring a doctor."

Matt had no intention of agreeing to that. "I have to trust my gut on this. Gideon, is Dominic Cordova behind this attack?"

"No. Dominic is working for us now. It wouldn't be in his interest to go after a federal agent," he said with absolute confidence. "What about Cassandra Harrison? Has she been in touch with you?"

He considered lying but decided to go for the truth, minus some pertinent details. "Yes. She believes Dominic framed her for murder."

"There's no proof of that, and Dominic says he's innocent."

"In other words, you'll believe him, or at least

pretend to believe him, and in doing so, you'll sacrifice Cass Harrison."

"It's not a sacrifice. All the evidence indicates that she's guilty."

"You know she's not."

His boss stayed quiet a moment. "I know what I have to do," Gideon countered. "And what I have to do is accept that departmental policy is what's best for everyone."

That turned his stomach. He glanced at Cass, and from the look in her eyes, she had the same reaction.

"Two questions," Matt continued. "Did you put together this deal with Dominic?"

"I was part of it, yes," Gideon readily admitted. "He's about to go into business with a man named Sylvester Marquez. He murdered two DEA agents, but he wasn't convicted because of some illegally processed evidence."

"And you can't try him again because of double jeopardy," Matt provided.

"That's right. But if Dominic closes this deal with Marquez, we'll have the business records we need to convict Marquez of tax evasion and at least a half-dozen other white-collar crimes that'll keep him in jail for the rest of his life."

"I understand the need to serve up justice to a killer," Matt continued, "but Dominic is a killer, too. And that begs the question—just how friendly are you with Dominic?"

"I don't even know the man." And he sounded riled that Matt had insinuated such a thing. "You're angry at the wrong person, Matt. I'm not responsible for what Cass Harrison did, and judging from the evidence, neither is Dominic Cordova."

Matt was about to try to change Gideon's mind about Dominic's innocence and value to the department, but he heard Cass's phone vibrate.

Cass looked down at the phone screen. "It's Hollis," she mouthed.

"Gideon, I'll have to call you back," Matt said. And he could hear the man's protests as he hung up.

"Hollis?" Cass answered in a whisper.

Matt watched her face, trying to figure out what was going on, but he didn't have to wait long. The call lasted mere seconds.

Cass put her mouth to his ear again. "Dominic is about to leave to go into town. Hollis bribed the guard at the garden room entrance to disappear for a while. Hollis says to come on foot. Don't use the car."

Matt didn't even question Hollis's instructions or how long *a while* would be. He grabbed his gun and his gear, and he put the jammer for the surveillance system into his pocket.

They'd need it.

Chapter Eight

Cass forced herself to focus on only one thing: getting inside the estate.

She had to push aside the concern, the danger, the latest kiss with Matt and the conversation she'd just overheard between Gideon and him.

Even though it stung.

Until now she truly hadn't thought Gideon was responsible for that leak in communication or the deal with Dominic. And why hadn't she thought that? Because she'd trusted him, that's why. Just as she'd trusted Dominic.

When was she going to learn?

Considering that she'd initiated that kiss with Matt, *never.*

She kicked a rock out of her path and continued the trek across the massive estate lawn. The wind, straight from the north, swiped at them. So did the drizzle. It wasn't cold enough to freeze, but it was close, and her discount store wool jacket wasn't much protection against a West Texas winter.

"I would ask if you're okay…" Matt said, walking beside her. He was cautious, keeping watch around them, but he was also glancing at the infrared screen so he could figure out where everyone was in the house.

"I'm not okay, but I'll live." Cass hoped. After all, they were headed into a lion's den, and even though the lion wouldn't be there, his guards would be. "For the record, I don't trust Gideon, Libby, Ronald or anyone in the Justice Department, present company excluded."

"Gideon is following policy line, but I don't believe he would do anything criminal."

She hoped her huff conveyed her skepticism.

Ahead of them she saw a man step from one of the delivery trucks parked on the grounds. It was Hollis, and he was carrying a cardboard box. Matt automatically slipped his hand into his jacket. No doubt so he could have easy access to his gun.

"We're a distrustful pair," she mumbled. "So, what's the plan here?"

"We go in through the garden room. I'll use the jammer so the surveillance cameras won't detect us. You can monitor the infrared thermal device to make sure no one sneaks up on us. Then, we can go to the basement so you can look for those surveillance disks."

Cass had to take a deep breath. After nearly a year on the run, it didn't seem possible that she was this close. But there was a flip side to this coin.

Matt's daughter.

"What about Molly?" she asked. "How do we rescue her?"

He tilted the infrared screen so she could see the three heat blobs in the nursery. "I'll keep watch while we're in the basement. Maybe they'll leave her alone so I can get into the room."

Cass had more questions, but they involved various scenarios of things that could go wrong. And that's why she didn't bother to ask them. Regardless of the possible scenarios, they had to be ready for anything once they stepped into the house.

"Christmas decorations," Hollis announced when he approached them. He handed the box to Cass. It was filled with gold tinsel and fresh holly. "If anyone asks, you're part of the crew."

Matt nodded. "How long before the guard returns?"

Hollis shook his head. "Don't know. Once you're in, you're on your own."

Yes. And those Christmas decorations wouldn't provide much protection against guards. For them to succeed, they'd need some luck to go along with the jammer and the infrared scanner.

Hollis turned to walk away, but Matt caught on to his arm. He was lightning quick and shoved up Hollis's sleeve to expose his wrist.

Or rather to expose a tattoo.

"A trident," Matt observed.

Hollis jerked his arm back and shoved down the sleeve of his jacket. "So?"

"You were a Navy SEAL," Matt pointed out.

"We all got a past of some kind," he mumbled. And he strolled away, in the direction of the front of the estate.

"Now, there's someone to trust," Matt said, sarcasm heavy.

Cass glanced at him. "You think being a Navy SEAL is a reason to distrust someone?"

"He's an *ex*-SEAL who's willing to take money to betray his boss. Not exactly a good character endorsement."

No. It wasn't. Not that Cass needed anything else to make her uneasy.

Matt nestled the infrared scanner amid the holly and tinsel in the box so that she could still easily see it, and they went to the garden room that jutted out from the east side of the house.

There was no one at the triple beveled-glass doors. Just as Hollis had said. Matt hit the jammer switch, and after he slipped the device back into his pocket, they went inside.

Instant warmth. Cass welcomed it, but went on even higher alert. They were inside, but they had a long way to go.

"This way," she instructed. When Cass had visited the estate, she'd been given a brief tour. Not of all the rooms, but she'd studied the floor plans that Hollis had given her, and she knew where the vault was.

More or less.

She glanced at the infrared screen. People were milling all around the place, but it appeared they had a clear path to the basement. She led Matt in that direction, through the garden room, into the back hall that was lavishly decorated like an Italian villa.

Cass could hear people talking from the other rooms. Someone was alarmed that the surveillance cameras weren't working. Hopefully, they wouldn't be able to figure out the problem anytime soon.

Matt and she went down the stairs. No ornate decor here. This was a place for storage, and Cass soon found the vault that she'd been looking for. It was at the end of the wide corridor with a concrete floor. She handed the box of decorations to Matt. Said a prayer. Pressed in the sequence of numbers that she'd bought from Hollis.

And the vault opened.

Cass didn't know whose breath of relief was louder—Matt's or hers. She got just a glimpse of the shelves of surveillance disks inside when she heard the sound.

Matt obviously heard it as well because he whirled around and reached for his gun.

"Don't move," the man said.

It was one of Dominic's uniformed guards. He was at the top of the stairs.

And he had an AK-47 aimed right at them.

"PUT DOWN THAT BOX," the gunman ordered. "And lift your hands so I can see them."

Matt purposely widened his eyes when he did a fake visual examination of the AK-47. What he was really doing was an examination of the gunman himself. Dressed in fatigues, steel-toed boots and with a take-no-prisoners formidable expression, he had his finger on the trigger.

Yep, the guy was ready and willing to shoot them.

Which meant Matt had to do something fast.

"You're not supposed to be down here," the man added in a snarl.

"We have orders to get last year's Christmas disks," Matt countered.

"Why?"

Matt shrugged. "I didn't ask."

It was the gunman's turn to study them. His iron-hard gaze went from the box-holding Matt to Cass. Matt shifted his position just slightly in case he had to go for his gun. Even though Cass had insisted that no one at the estate other than Dominic would recognize her, there was always the possibility that someone on Dominic's staff might remember her from her short visit nearly a year ago. Matt didn't want a shootout here inside the estate, but he wasn't going to stand by and let this goon kill them, either.

Time crawled by.

Finally the guard snapped, "Make it quick."

Oh, they intended to do that. Matt nudged Cass into the vault ahead of him, and he stayed near the doorway so he could keep watch in case the guard decided to call someone to report them or in case he decided to take a closer look.

Thankfully, Cass didn't waste any time. She hurried along the long rows of shelves, mumbling the dates that she read off the spines of the plastic storage cases. She stopped, pulled out several and shoved them into the box that she took from him.

"Hurry up!" the guard called out.

And that barked order made Matt consider their next possible dilemma. What if the guard wanted to check the surveillance disks? The dates were close enough that he might believe they were Christmas disks, but if the man took a good look, Cass and he would be in real danger of being killed on the spot.

Knowing what he had to do, Matt eased his hand over his gun so it'd be ready if he needed it.

Matt went out ahead of Cass. "Don't shut the vault door all the way," he whispered to her.

Their eyes met, and he saw that she understood. They might have to use the room for cover in the event of a shootout.

Matt walked toward the stairs, keeping a close eye on the guard. He'd only made it a few steps when he heard another shout.

"Buck?" someone called out. "Get in here now. I just found a switchblade on one of the morons decorating the Christmas tree."

The guard turned toward the voice. Cursed viciously.

And he shot Matt a warning glance before he turned and left.

Matt didn't wait for his heartbeat to return to normal. That wouldn't happen while they were in the estate, anyway. Cass and he started up the stairs.

"Oh, no," Cass mumbled.

Matt immediately looked for another guard, but he soon realized it wasn't a guard that'd caused her reaction. She was staring at the infrared monitor.

"Molly's no longer in the nursery," Cass informed him. "There's just one adult in there. Judging from her posture, it looks like Annette sitting in her wheelchair."

Matt had a look for himself. Cass was right. No small color mass to indicate a baby. He frantically looked through the rest of the house.

There was no sign of Molly.

"We're going to the nursery," Matt informed her. Yes, it was a risk, but someway, somehow he had to figure out what'd happened to his daughter.

There was a guard in the hall. Not Buck, the one who'd held them at gunpoint. This was a bulky Hispanic guy who barely gave them a second glance. He was obviously a man on a mission because he was hurrying in the direction of the garden room. Even though the guy was likely cutting off their exit, Matt and Cass went in the opposite direction.

It was like a maze to get to the nursery. Three halls. Three turns. At least a dozen rooms. Cass navigated them all from memory of studying the plans Hollis had given her. Along the way, Matt checked the jammer to make sure it was still working.

It was.

Thankfully the corridor just outside the nursery was empty and the door was ajar. With his hand still on his gun, he peeked inside, and came face-to-face with Annette Cordova.

The woman wasn't in a wheelchair. It was several feet away, and she had walking canes in each hand.

"Good," Annette said immediately. "You're here. I asked Dominic to keep me updated about the trip, but I wasn't sure he would. Has Molly left yet?"

That sent Matt's heart to his knees. "I don't know. Where is she?"

The woman was obviously distraught. Her eyes were red, and her bottom lip was trembling. "She's on the way to the doctor, of course. I thought that was why you were here, to give me an update."

Matt's heart stayed at his knees, and he shook his head. "I'm sorry, but I don't know anything about the trip." He tried to sound casually interested but not too interested. "Is Molly sick or something?"

"No. She needs her six-month checkup. I wanted to go, but Dominic wouldn't let me. He sent the nanny with her instead." Annette blinked away a fresh round of tears. "You don't know if they've left yet?"

"No," Cass answered.

Annette looked at her as if she'd just realized Cass was there. And Matt held his breath. Cass had never met Annette, but that didn't mean she hadn't seen photos of Cass and Dominic when they were together. Annette's eyes narrowed slightly.

Matt tightened his grip on his gun.

He couldn't kill or even hurt this woman. Not even if she recognized Cass. But that recognition could mean he was going to have to *convince* Annette to let them out of there.

"You're part of Buck's crew?" Annette asked. Her eyes narrowed even more. "Because I don't remember ever seeing you around before, and he doesn't usually hire women."

"We're working for Hollis. Temporary seasonal help," Matt added. He tipped his head to the box of Christmas decorations and was glad that the barely five-feet-tall Annette was too short to see the monitor and disk nestled in the tinsel.

"Yes," Annette said softly. Almost regretfully. No more narrow-eyed glares. "I said something to Dominic about wanting a big Christmas for Molly, and I think he went a little overboard. Well, actually it's for his big Christmas Eve party, but he's telling everyone that it's for Molly."

Thankfully he had gone overboard, because the decorations had already saved their butts.

"I'm sure Molly will be all right," Cass volunteered. "The nanny's with her so it's not as if she'll be alone."

Annette nodded. A no-faith kind of nod, and she turned away to return to her wheelchair. "Dominic doesn't like it when I use the canes. He thinks it puts too much stress on my legs," she said, tucking the canes beneath a cheery strawberry-pink sofa.

The sofa matched everything else in the room. The crib. A fuzzy beanbag type chair. Even most of the toys were pink as was the painted desk in the corner near the fireplace.

"We could maybe follow the chauffeur," Matt suggested. "If you're worried about Molly's safety."

"It's not her safety that concerns me. Not at this minute anyway," she added in a mumble. "Dominic's sending his men with her, at least three of them, he promised. And they'll protect her with their lives. But she might be scared at the doctor's office, and I wanted to be with her."

The relief that Matt felt was a little overwhelming. His daughter was okay. Annette was just being motherly.

"When will Molly be back?" Cass asked.

"Not until sometime tomorrow on Christmas Eve. Her new doctor is in El Paso, over a hundred miles away. Dominic wouldn't give me the name because he's afraid I'll go after her. And I would. He says I can't. That my health's not good enough to be out in this cold and that I'm too devoted to her. He says I need to back off and stop smothering her. I can't believe he'd think that. My health is fine, and I love Molly."

Well, that last part was the one good thing Matt wanted to hear. "So, where exactly is Molly now? Do you think they've left the estate?"

"Probably. In fact, they're likely at the airfield ready to take off in Dominic's jet."

Matt's relief vanished.

His daughter was about to be airborne en route to the doctor. Cass and he could drive to El Paso, but without the name of the pediatrician, it'd be a needle in a haystack search. The only thing good was that if Molly was truly in El Paso, it meant Annette couldn't whisk her out of the country.

"Molly will be back tomorrow," Cass said as if comforting Annette.

But Matt knew she was really comforting him.

And she was also reminding him that it'd be tomorrow before he could take his child and get away from the estate. Matt had no choice but to agree. However, he didn't get a chance to voice that agreement because something caught his attention. He spotted the silver-framed picture over the mantel.

It was Molly. Her face beaming, the smile so bright that Matt could feel it.

Annette must have followed his gaze, and she smiled. "I just had that picture taken last week. Isn't she a sweetheart?"

Matt was sorely tempted to try to take the photo, but it would be a stupid risk. Besides, the picture was a paltry substitute for the real thing, and with luck, tomorrow he'd have his daughter.

"Do you have children?" Annette asked Matt.

He nodded. "A daughter."

Annette returned the nod. "Then, you know how I feel."

"I do."

They shared a glance and a quiet moment. "I haven't properly introduced myself, even though you probably know who I am—Annette Cordova."

"Bill," Matt lied. "And this is Sandy."

"Well, it's nice to meet you. I'm sure you both miss your little girl as much as I miss mine."

Matt settled for a semi-grunt. Odd, that Annette had considered Cass and him to be parents. A couple. He hoped they weren't emanating something that would make others think that. Best for everyone at the estate to believe they were workers and nothing else.

Outside in the hall, he could hear two men. They were discussing the problem with the security system. Judging from the snatches of what Matt heard, Dominic had been called and was on his way back.

Cass and he had to get out of there. Annette didn't know Cass, but Dominic did. One glimpse of her, and he would likely order the guards to kill them.

"You must think I'm spineless," Annette said, just as Matt was ready to say goodbye.

"No." Cass took a few steps toward her. "But it sounds as if you need help."

Annette's breath shuddered. She opened her mouth. Closed it. And looked up at the tiny surveillance camera mounted in the corner of the room. "I'm sorry. I misspoke. I said things I shouldn't have said. It's because I'm tired. I didn't sleep very well last night."

The woman was obviously afraid that Dominic or one of his men was listening. Ironic, since Matt had used the jammer to prevent the possibility of that happening. Still, he couldn't very well confess that tidbit to Dominic's sister, because he couldn't trust her. But Annette was a woman practically begging for help.

Help that Matt wanted to give her.

If he knew this wasn't some kind of act. Heck, she was Dominic's sister, and this could be her way of ferreting out untrustworthy employees.

But Matt had seen her cry earlier in the garden room.

Annette hadn't known anyone was watching her, and those tears did not look fake.

Still…

"I'll give you my cell number," Cass volunteered. She passed Matt the box, used a small strip of paper and a pen from the pink desk to write down the number. She pressed it into Annette's hand. "Call me if you think there's anything I can do to help."

"There's no reason to call. Everything's fine," Annette said. But her hand closed in a tight fist around the slip of paper with Cass's cell phone number.

"Let's go," Matt insisted. "We need to put up these decorations."

Cass gave Annette a reassuring glance before she took the box from him and headed out.

"Dominic's on his way back," Matt whispered to her.

That caused Cass to move a little faster. They threaded their way through the hall maze and went to the garden room. The guard was there, as Matt had expected. Other than a nod, Matt offered the man no greeting.

And no explanation.

Matt figured if they looked as if they belonged there, then the guy wouldn't try to stop them.

It worked.

He glanced at the gold tinsel dangling over the edge of the box, returned Matt's nod and actually opened the door for them. Still keeping with the we-belong-here act, Cass and he didn't hurry, though it was still cold and drizzling. They practically strolled across the yard.

Until Matt heard the footsteps.

Buck stepped out from a cluster of Texas sage bushes. He wasn't armed with an AK-47 this time but with an equally lethal Glock that was rigged with a silencer. "I've been watching for you two. Now, mind telling me who the hell you are?"

"We're part of the crew that's decorating the place for Christmas," Matt offered.

Buck shook his head. "I just went through the pictures of all the temporary hired help, and your faces aren't there. That's real bad news for you two. I have orders from Dominic to shoot any and all trespassers."

That was the only warning Buck gave them before he pulled the trigger.

Chapter Nine

One second Cass was on her feet, wondering what in the name of heaven they were going to do.

The next second she was on the slippery cold ground where Matt had shoved her.

He fell on the ground, too, just as the silenced bullet swooshed past them.

A second shot quickly followed. Matt had a quick response to that, as well—he shoved her on the other side of a thick Texas sage bush.

Then Matt came up ready to fire.

Or at least that's what Cass thought he was going to do until he tossed his gun aside and launched himself at Buck. Matt tackled the man, and his momentum sent them both flying backward.

Cass retrieved Matt's gun, shoved it into her coat pocket and scrambled toward them so she could help. But all she could see was a tangle of body parts.

The fight was obviously on for Buck's gun, and Cass figured out why Matt hadn't just shot the man when he had the chance. Matt's gun wasn't rigged with a silencer. One blast from his Glock, and the sound would alert Dominic's men.

All of them.

A blast like that would have essentially meant that Matt and she would be killed. This way, they had a chance.

The wrestling match turned into a fist fight. Cass tried to maneuver herself into a position to get Buck's gun. She also tried to keep watch of their surroundings to make sure no one had noticed the disturbance.

Matt slammed his forearm into the other man's jaw. Buck's head flopped back, but what he didn't do was let go of the gun. He did manage to recover quickly enough to land a wicked punch to Matt's jaw. The men were obviously a close match in body size and skill, and Cass couldn't take the risk that Buck would win.

She dove at Buck. Specifically at his right hand and the gun. Cass caught a knee in the thigh, and the impact shot pain through her. She ignored it and kept moving so she could latch on to his wrist. It didn't do her any good. As if she had zero strength, Buck slung off her grip, and instead of Cass retrieving the gun, it bashed her in the cheek.

This time, the pain was a little harder to ignore.

Still, she forced herself to do just that because this fight had to end here and now before they were detected by one of the other guards.

Cass kicked at the gun. No success. The men exchanged blows again, and she saw the blood on Matt's mouth. They rolled over the ground, both men jockeying for position. Cass jockeyed, too, and this time she aimed her kick at Buck's elbow.

Buck yelled in pain.

Which meant time was running out fast since anyone could have heard it.

But her kick caused the man to loosen his grip on the gun, and Matt was able to wrench it from his hand. Temporarily. Buck locked his hands around the gun, too, and a new fight was on.

She saw a finger on the trigger, but before Cass could determine whose finger it was, she heard the sound. The swoosh.

Someone had pulled the trigger.

She bit her lip to stop herself from shouting, but she couldn't do much to stop the horrifying feeling that slammed through her.

Mercy, was Matt hurt?

Someone in the body heap moved. She couldn't tell if it was Matt or Buck. She forced herself to do something, so she could help Matt. And all the while she prayed that help wasn't necessary.

More movement. She saw the blood. God, there was a lot of blood, and it was soaked across the front of Matt's shirt. Cass knelt beside him. Still praying.

And that's when she realized Buck wasn't moving.

Matt shoved the man off him, and Cass soon realized the source of the blood. It was definitely coming from

Buck. Or rather *had* come from him. She pressed her fingers to his neck and found not even a trace of a pulse.

"He's dead," Matt informed her. With his breath coming out in rough gusts, he stood, caught Buck and began to drag him toward the sage bushes. "We have to hide the body."

Cass nodded and knew she had to help him. Matt was right, of course. Buck had tried to kill them and was now dead himself. Calling 911 or an ambulance wouldn't help, and a call like that would mean they wouldn't be able to rescue Molly. Still, Cass's stomach turned when she grabbed the dead man's hand and helped Matt pull Buck into the shrubs. Thankfully, the bushes were thick enough to hide him.

Now she only hoped that no one had seen them.

She did a quick search around them. Matt grabbed the box of Christmas decorations, disks and equipment.

"Let's go," Matt insisted.

He didn't have to tell her twice. Cass was more than anxious to put some distance between herself and the body. She felt herself tremble. It didn't stay a tremble, either. By the time she made it to the stone cottage, she was shaking from head to toe.

"My clothes are damp," she mumbled to Matt when he gave her a questioning glance.

He shut the door, locked it and stared at her. He obviously didn't believe that was the reason she was shaking.

Cass didn't believe it, either.

In fact, she was having a hard time believing what had just happened. But the proof was all over Matt's face and clothes. His lip was bleeding, and there was a cut on his forehead. Plus, there was all that blood on his shirt and jacket. He peeled off both items, tossed the jacket over the back of the chair. The shirt went in the kitchen sink.

"I can't burn it," he whispered. He reached down and turned the small space heater on high. "Someone might see the smoke and get curious."

She nodded. Just nodded. And she watched while he doused the shirt with bleach and dishwashing liquid that he took from beneath the sink. Because she had to do something, anything, to occupy her mind, she grabbed a rag from the counter and wiped the blood off his jacket.

"Are you okay?" he asked.

Cass was about to answer "sure," but her teeth began to chatter. Great. Now, she was trembling and chattering. "I've never seen a dead man," she admitted.

"Yeah. I figured that out." He left the shirt to soak, dried his hands and went to her. Matt pulled her into his arms. "We did what we had to do back there."

"I know. I just regret that it had to happen in the first place." She was so weary. So drained, both physically and emotionally. And Cass allowed her head to drop onto his shoulder. "I thought I was tough because I'd been on the run for so long. But I'm not tough."

"You kicked a hired gun. That's tough."

"I was afraid he was going to kill you."

He pulled back slightly. Looked down at her. He pushed the hair from her face and smiled. "You'll have a bruise on your cheek."

She could feel the sting of it. Ditto for the spot on her thigh where she'd been kicked. "You have a cut on the corner of your mouth," she let him know. But she definitely didn't return his smile.

She hoped he would say something light and even smart-mouthed to break the wave of emotion flooding her body. But he didn't. He leaned in and kissed her.

And he immediately winced.

"The cut on your mouth," she reminded him.

But he didn't heed the reminder. He kissed her again.

This time he didn't wince.

Neither did she.

Cass felt that kick that she desperately wanted. His kiss broke the wave of emotion inside her. She could feel the tension drain from her and the heat spread through every inch of her. Until she wasn't cold. Until she wasn't shivering. It was warm and comforting. Like snuggling with a familiar blanket.

Until she realized he wasn't wearing a shirt.

His bare chest was against her. And his bare arms were holding her. There was nothing, however, bare about his kiss. Despite the cut lip, Matt was doing an adequate job of heating her up from head to toe. And Cass did absolutely nothing to stop him.

In fact, she was the one who escalated things.

She pressed herself against him, drawing on the warmth from his skin, his strength. All she wanted to do was forget the terrible images of the guard's death. She didn't want to feel the pain, the weariness or the dread. She only wanted to forget.

When she pressed against Matt, he pressed right back. He pushed her against the wall, holding her in place with his body while his mouth took hers as if he owned her.

And for this moment, he did.

The wild kisses got even hotter when his mouth went to her neck. Cass reacted to the not-so-gentle coaxing of his tongue. She melted. The heat kicked up a notch, and the ache escalated.

She angled her hips against him, seeking some kind of relief from the heat and the ache. Matt accommodated her unspoken request. He hooked his arm around her waist and lifted her, wrapping her legs around him until the center of her body met the center of his.

The fit was so perfect that it took her breath away.

She slipped her hands between them to reach his zipper. Cass encountered a very aroused man on her quest, and she was ready to wrap her fingers around him. But Matt moved her hand away.

"I need to keep watch," he said.

That didn't make any sense to her, until she noticed

that while he was racking her body with pleasure, he was also glancing out the window.

"Talk about multitasking," Cass mumbled. "This is crazy, Matt. We should stop."

But she didn't want to stop. Still, she knew this situation was out of control and had the worst timing possible. So, that meant she had to do the right thing and call it quits. She would have, too, if Matt hadn't taken multitasking to the next level.

He went after her zipper.

Cass was about to tell him that she could stand watch, too, but she suddenly couldn't speak. He inched her zipper down, and his hands went in her panties.

Just like that, without nearly enough warning, he touched her in the one spot that could render her speechless. He used his fingers to send her flying.

Cass would have preferred a different part of Matt for the penetrating task—but after a few of those clever finger strokes, she was satisfied with what he was doing. Those maddening fingers slid through her slippery heat and created the friction that both soothed and fed the ache that was now raging inside her.

Matt didn't stop. He didn't slow down.

Cass didn't even try to fight to hang on to the pleasure a while longer. She couldn't. Everything was moving too fast until it was speeding out of control, exactly the way she wanted.

Matt's clever fingers and kisses sent her over the edge.

And when she fell, he was right there to catch her.

She had to wait a moment, just to gather enough breath to speak. And even then Cass kept it simple.

"Your turn."

Chapter Ten

Matt skipped his turn.

And now his body was making him pay for it.

Unfulfilled need was a bear to deal with, and in his case it just kept on coming. It'd been hours since his encounter with Cass, and he'd given up good old-fashioned mental suppression and opted for the cold shower.

It didn't help, either, but that was asking a lot from a shower.

So he stepped from the shower stall, dried off, dressed in his jeans and spare shirt and tried to figure out what the hell he was going to say to Cass. What did you say to a woman after you'd had your hands in her pants? He'd acted like a teenager, and that had to stop. He had to stay focused on the mission.

Bolstered by his mental lecture, Matt took a deep breath and came out of the bathroom.

The first thing he heard was Cass's sigh.

Matt figured that wasn't a good sign, especially

since she was on the bed, volleying her attention between keeping watch out the window and reviewing Dominic's security disks on his laptop.

She'd been looking at those disks for hours, since her own shower after their spontaneous make-out session. And other than those sighs, she wasn't communicating much.

But then, neither was he.

Matt had considered apologizing. Heck, he'd even considered discussing the situation. But the truth was, there was no discussion needed. He'd violated a personal rule or two by giving her some release, but he damn sure didn't regret it. That climax had stopped her trembling. It'd gotten her mind off the dead guy. If he had it to do all over again, he wouldn't change a thing.

Well, except maybe finishing what he'd started.

That would have violated more than a rule or two, but with that slow hard ache in his body and the way she'd responded to it, it'd be worth some rule violations.

But since thinking about sex with Cass only made him want her more, he forced his mind back on his task, surveillance.

He grabbed the binoculars, and as he'd done most of the afternoon and early evening, he looked for any sign that someone had found the body they'd hidden in the shrubs. Or that someone was on the way to the cottage. But no one was headed their way.

It was just Cass and him.

He took his place in the chair right in front of the window, reached behind him and grabbed an energy bar from the food stash they'd bought on the drive to the estate. The bar would be dinner. He'd already had one for lunch, and since it was the energy bars or nothing, he would be having another one for breakfast.

"Any activity at the estate while I was in the shower?" he asked.

"Definitely not Molly and the nanny."

But then, he knew they wouldn't be returning tonight—he'd verified that by contacting the airfield that the pilot had used to fly to El Paso. He'd pretended to be someone on Dominic's staff, and had learned that the return flight wasn't until 8:00 a.m. It'd be at least another ten hours before he could see his daughter.

"I didn't see any signs of anyone looking for Buck, thank goodness," she added. "A limo arrived about fifteen minutes ago, but I think it might be a guest who came in a day early for the party."

Matt figured there'd be a lot of limos and luxury cars arriving soon. That wasn't a bad thing. The guests would provide good cover.

"How about you?" Matt asked. "Anything on those disks?"

"No. The dates on them are the right time frame, but there's no footage of Dominic's office. There's especially no footage of Dominic shooting his business associate, Arthur Wilmer."

"And you're sure Dominic has surveillance in his

office?" Matt asked, keeping his voice as soft as possible.

"Positive. He even showed me the cameras and said they were there because he didn't trust his employees. He told me he wanted proof of anything and everything that went on under his roof." She paused. "But I'm not positive that the disk of the murder still exists. Dominic could have destroyed it."

Matt was afraid of that, too. "What about another way to verify that he killed Wilmer? Other witnesses, maybe?"

She shook her head. "I was the only semiwitness who wasn't on Dominic's payroll, and I don't think Dominic would have kept the gun."

No. But there were other ways to leave evidence. "Tell me what happened that day."

Another sigh. She scrapped her thumbnail over a loose thread on her jeans. "Dominic brought me to the estate for what was supposed to be lunch and a tour of the place. I'd only been there an hour or so when Arthur arrived."

"You knew him, right?"

She nodded. "We were joint investors in a project a few months earlier. It hadn't gone well. Arthur was a crook. Dominic and Arthur started to argue immediately. And Dominic took him into his office. A few minutes later I heard the shot. I started to go in, but then one of Dominic's guards came running out of the office. He said I killed Arthur and that Dominic was calling the police."

So, it'd been a setup. "What'd you do then?"

"I tried to do what any reasonable person would do—talk to Dominic because I thought there was some kind of misunderstanding. But I heard him actually call the sheriff. His head of security came down the hall, grabbed me and shoved me into a room. He locked the door. When I realized what was happening, that I was about to be framed for murder, I managed to escape through the window."

"Dominic probably wanted you to escape," Matt mumbled.

The only illumination was coming from the outside light and the computer monitor, but he had no trouble seeing that info register in her expression. "Because if I escaped, it made me look even guiltier. Plus, I wasn't there to give my side of the story."

Matt nodded. "If it's any consolation, Dominic would have found a reason to kill you before the sheriff got there. According to Ronald, Sheriff Medina isn't in Dominic's pocket, so Dominic would have gotten rid of you before the start of an investigation."

She groaned, scrubbed her hands over her face and then winced when she made contact with her bruised cheek. "I was really an idiot to ever trust Dominic."

"Ah, that hindsight stuff again." Matt picked up an energy bar and was about to toss it to her, but she declined it with a head shake. "There's a bright side to this. You need to look for a surveillance disk of the hall outside Dominic's office. Because that's where you were when the shooting occurred, and the disk will prove it."

She smiled, but it quickly faded. "If Dominic didn't destroy that one."

"We'll know when we get back in there tomorrow."

"Yes. After Molly returns." She set the laptop on the nightstand, and slipped her legs and feet under the covers. She rubbed her obviously chilly hands. "We might not have time to look for the disk and take Molly, too."

"We'll take Molly," he insisted. He tossed the energy bar back into the equipment bag.

"We will," Cass agreed. "Even if it means not getting the disk."

Matt stared at her. Oh, man. That was what he wanted her to say, but he wasn't necessarily glad to hear it. He knew the implications, and those implications were huge. "Does this have anything to do with what happened between us earlier?"

"No." But she dodged his gaze as if she weren't so certain of that *no*. "We can't leave her in there any longer. I wish there was a way to intercept the nanny on the way home from the airport."

"Too risky." Matt had already given it plenty of thought. "Those guards will start shooting, and I can't risk Molly being hit. Our best bet is to take her from the nursery, get back to the car and drive out of here before anyone knows she's missing."

A lot of things could go wrong, but he wasn't going

to dwell on that. Tomorrow, he would have his daughter. And Cass still might not have the evidence to keep her out of jail.

Of course he would do what he could to help her. Matt only hoped it would be enough.

"You're dreading going to bed, aren't you?" she whispered.

Because he was mentally going through tomorrow's rescue, it took Matt a moment to figure out what Cass said.

And what she meant.

There was only one bed, and it wasn't big enough for both of them. Heck, a whole furniture store of beds wouldn't be big enough because they just kept finding their way into each other's arms.

Not good.

They had the mother of all missions ahead of them.

"I'll sleep on the floor," he let her know.

She pulled the cover up to her chin. "That tile and the room are cold. There's only one blanket. You're not sleeping on the floor. You're sleeping here on the bed with me."

"You think that's wise?"

"No," she readily admitted. "We just have to be adult about it."

Matt felt himself frown. "It's because we're grown-up that we can't be adult about it."

She laughed. Actually laughed. And it made him wonder how long it'd been since that had happened.

Probably over a year ago before Dominic turned her life upside down.

That riled Matt.

Dominic hadn't just taken his daughter; he'd taken away a year of Cass's life. Even if she was exonerated and cleared of all charges, she'd never get back that year, and she'd never be the same.

Dominic would pay for that.

Matt glanced at the cold floor. Then at Cass. She was sitting there, in bed, waiting. She certainly wasn't dressed provocatively. She was wearing a dull gray flannel shirt and jeans. No makeup. And her hair framed the delicate features of her face.

She didn't look like a pampered heiress. She looked hot and welcoming.

Matt knew that was a bad combination. He grabbed his gun and the infrared scanner and put them on the metal nightstand next to their cell phones. That way, he could at least watch out for approaching *visitors* while he tortured himself with what he was about to do.

And what he was about to do was get in that bed with a woman that he wanted more than his next breath.

Definitely torture.

But that didn't stop him. When Cass lifted the covers, he climbed right in.

Matt had been right about the size of the bed. Not big enough for both. So, he stayed on his side. Not facing Cass. She stayed on her side, too, facing his back. Snuggled together, because there wasn't room to have even a sliver of space between them.

"About what happened earlier…" she whispered.

"Don't finish that."

"Why?"

Matt opted for a nonverbal, crude explanation. He grabbed her hand and put it over his aroused body. Just as quickly, he moved it away.

"Oh," she said. And Cass repeated it, causing her warm breath to brush over the back of his neck. It was almost as effective as her touching him. "My body's doing the same thing. I could take your hand and show you the proof, but—"

"Don't finish that, either," Matt snarled. "Look, I haven't had sex in months, and I'm in bed with a woman I find very attractive. I have to keep reminding myself why it wouldn't be a good idea to strip you out of those jeans and sink deep and hard into you."

Somehow, she managed to snuggle even closer. "And remind me why we can't have sex?"

He groaned. "Because it would be a distraction, and in this bed, possibly even suicide."

"Well, I could do to you what you did to me earlier," she volunteered.

It was tempting. But he couldn't even consider it. "It'd still be a distraction, especially for me."

"Thinking about having sex with you is a distraction, too," she mumbled. And it sounded a lot like an invitation.

"A little one. Trust me, if I do to you what I'd love to do, it wouldn't be a little distraction. Plus, we don't have a condom."

Cass cleared her throat. "There are several in the equipment bag."

He groaned again. Yes, there were, but he didn't want to be reminded of them. They weren't just tempting, they were adding to his torture. It wasn't unusual for agents to have them in the equipment bags, along with toothpaste, soap, bug repellant, painkillers and even extra underwear, but Matt wished that Ronald had taken the time to remove the condoms.

"Try to get some sleep," Matt told her. Then he thought about sleep, and the bed. "I'll try not to roll over, either, or we might accidentally have sex."

She laughed again, and he smiled at the sound.

But not for long.

Cass's cell phone buzzed. Before he could reach for it, she crawled over him, answered it and clicked the speaker function so they could both hear the caller.

"It's me," the man said.

Hollis.

It probably wasn't a good thing that he was calling this time of night, so Matt automatically reached for his gun.

"What's wrong?" Cass immediately asked the man.

"Some guy named Timothy St. Claire arrived a little while ago. Annette and he are pen pals. They met on the Internet."

Cass made a sound of concern. "You know this man?"

"No. And judging from their conversation, tonight's the first time Annette has met him. Don't know how long they've been e-mailing or how close they are. I listened in on what they had to say, and St. Claire's going to help Annette sneak Molly out of the house tomorrow evening just as the party is in full swing. That way, they think they can get past Dominic."

Matt processed that. It didn't change his plan to rescue Molly ASAP, but it did mean they had someone else to watch since Timothy St. Claire might be on the lookout for potential glitches in their plan to take Molly out of the country. Either St. Claire was a complete idiot or else he didn't know about Dominic, because he was taking his life into his hands by helping Annette.

"If you want a look at this guy, he's in the garden room," Hollis added, and he hung up.

Matt did indeed want a look at the man he was up against. He also wanted to run a background check on him. After all, Dominic could have hired St. Claire to test his sister's loyalty.

And if so, his sister was about to fail big-time.

Annette had to be truly desperate to get Molly out if she was willing to trust a man she'd met over the Internet. She must have believed that Dominic's new business partner could provide a real threat to Molly's safety. Or maybe it was just a matter of the possibility that the unpredictable Dominic could on a whim take

Molly from her. Of course Matt understood that desperation. He was willing to let Cass risk her life to help him.

He took the binoculars to the window, zoomed in on the garden room and focused the lens. He spotted Annette in her wheelchair right away, and behind her was a dark-haired man dressed in a crisp black suit. His back was turned, and he appeared to be examining a large flowering plant in a terra-cotta pot.

"You see him?" Cass asked.

"He's there, just where Hollis said he would be, and he's talking to Annette."

"You think this guy is legit?"

"Don't know yet. Go ahead and do a computer search on him to see what pops up." Matt was about to add that he would search, as well, once he had a good look at him.

But the guy turned around, and Matt got that good look he'd wanted.

His stomach clenched into a knot. Because the man was someone that Matt knew all too well.

It was his boss, Gideon Tate.

Chapter Eleven

Cass kept watch out the window—something she'd been doing on and off most of the night, though she'd managed to get a few hours sleep.

She wasn't sure Matt had done the same.

Their "cozy" time in bed had been pitifully short indeed because the moment Matt spotted Gideon getting chummy with Annette, bedtime, rest and even basic conversation was over. Matt had spent most of the night either doing surveillance or trying to call Gideon and Ronald to see what was going on.

And he still didn't have answers.

Matt hadn't been able to reach Gideon. That wasn't exactly a surprise. And Ronald claimed to have no idea why Gideon was at Dominic's estate. Cass wasn't sure she believed the man, but then she'd been skeptical about trusting Ronald right from the start.

Gideon, however, was a different matter.

Cass *had* trusted him initially. Because of the old ties to her father. But that last time she'd called him, it'd only confirmed the breach in communication. She didn't know if Gideon was responsible for that or if someone else was. Still, it didn't look good for Gideon, especially since he was now at Dominic's estate pretending to be Annette's pen pal.

What was he doing?

Cass and Matt had followed the man with infrared until he retired for the night in one of the estate's many guest rooms. According to the monitor, he was in the breakfast room now, and he appeared to be with Annette.

"No sign of Molly?" Matt asked.

She glanced over his shoulder. He was still pounding away on the laptop keyboard. Still searching for answers, and judging from his scowl, he wasn't any closer to those answers than he had been hours ago.

"No Molly yet, just guards, but I'll scan any incoming vehicles with the infrared."

"How many guards?" Matt asked.

"Four, maybe five. They appear to be checking the perimeter of the house. In other words, it's not a good time to try to get into the estate."

Matt nodded. "But I want us to go in as soon as Molly arrives," he insisted. "Even if the guards are still there, we'll have to bluff our way in. And we can bring the infrared with us and hide out until we can take her from the nursery."

Cass waited for him to add more about Gideon's presence. When he didn't, she said what they were both no doubt thinking. "Gideon could be using Annette to get to Dominic."

"Perhaps. In part, anyway."

She hadn't expected that. Nor was she certain she would like what it meant. "You have a different theory?"

Matt stopped, lifted his head and met her gaze. "I don't doubt that someone in the department has been cultivating a relationship with Annette or Dominic. Any number of agents could be doing the actual e-mails as Timothy St. Claire, and Gideon could have stepped into the role because he felt it was the right time to do that. It could even be related to Dominic's new business partner."

Cass gave that some thought and watched on the infrared monitor as Gideon walked from the breakfast room, leaving his companion, Annette, alone.

"Gideon's on the move," she relayed to Matt. And she continued to mull over what Matt had just told her. "Since Gideon is a director in the department, is it normal for him to go into an actual undercover assignment?"

"It's never happened the entire time I've worked for him."

"Oh." She watched the images as Gideon went down the hall toward the garden room. "So, what does this mean?"

Matt shook his head. "I hope to hell he's not here because of Molly. Because he wants to help me by getting her out of the estate."

"Wouldn't that be good?" she asked.

"Not for you. Because then it's my guess that Gideon will want to deal. I'll get Molly if I turn you in."

That required Cass to take a deep breath. "I see."

"Don't worry. My goal is to get Molly before Annette and Gideon do."

That was Cass's goal too, but maybe Gideon wouldn't cooperate with that. It certainly complicated things that Gideon might be involved in the worst kind of way.

"Gideon just went outside," she told Matt. She switched from the infrared to the binoculars. "And it's not exactly the weather for a morning stroll. He's making a call."

And in the seconds that followed, Matt's phone rang. He immediately reached over, grabbed his phone from the nightstand and looked at the screen.

"Libby," he said answering in a whisper.

Not Gideon. Cass didn't know whether to be disappointed or not. She wished she could read lips so she would know whom Gideon had called.

Matt said little to his fellow agent, so Cass couldn't tell what had precipitated the call. Instead she focused on Gideon. He was walking now. Away from the estate. She lost sight of him when he disappeared into the formal gardens, and she switched back to infrared.

Matt's profanity caught her attention. "I don't want any of you coming here to the cottage."

Matt cursed some more, stabbed the end call button and hurried to the window. He brought his gun with him.

"Please tell me they're not all here," Cass whispered.

"Libby says Gideon bribed Hollis to get Ronald and her onto the estate. The three of them want to come here and talk to me."

Good grief. Just what they didn't need. "How did they even know you were here?"

"Ronald decided to confess all. They know Molly is my daughter."

"And do they know I'm here?" she asked.

"You're not here. Get your things and go into the bathroom."

It seemed too little too late. "They've probably already scanned the cottage with infrared."

"That doesn't mean they know you're the one who's here." He took her shoulders. "Cass, they'll try to arrest you if they see you."

"They might try to arrest you, too."

"That's not going to happen. They're not going to want to cause a scene on the estate. And if they'd already ratted me out to Dominic, then we'd be under attack from his guards."

Cass hoped that was true. But Matt was right. There was no sense flaunting her presence. Besides, Matt might get them to say more if she wasn't around. And she could intercede if their nonarrest theory failed and if the trio tried to haul Matt away.

She took her phone, jacket and gun and raced into the bathroom, but Cass left the door open just a sliver so she could hear the encounter that was about to take place.

She didn't have to wait long.

Matt kept a firm grip on his gun, and he opened the front door. By using the reflection in the bathroom mirror, Cass could see Ronald, Libby and Gideon as they approached the cottage. She could also see Matt's stiff, defensive posture. If Matt had had any trust left for them, he wasn't showing it.

"What are you doing here?" Matt demanded.

"I'm on official business," Gideon answered.

"By pretending to befriend Annette Cordova? And don't bother to ask how I know. I know."

Gideon was equally defensive and stiff. "You're aware of departmental policy regarding Dominic. I'll do whatever it takes to keep his trust."

"We're here to help you, Matt. We want to talk you out of doing something that could get you killed," Libby added. It sounded to Cass as if she was playing the "good cop," and her boss was going for "bad."

"You're not going to talk me out of anything," Matt returned. Cass watched as he shifted his position. "Ronald, I can't believe you of all people did this."

Ronald lifted his shoulder but had the decency to look apologetic and even sorry. "I thought I was helping."

"Well, you're not."

"Ronald was doing what any agent sworn to duty should do," Gideon said. "You'll do the same. Leave with Ronald and Libby now, or I'll put you on suspension."

"Then put me on suspension."

That didn't surprise Cass one bit. Even though he'd yet to meet Molly, Matt was totally committed to her and her rescue.

"I'm not leaving without my daughter," Matt continued, his voice low and dangerous now. "But you are."

Gideon took a step closer to Matt. "What does that mean?"

Matt stepped closer, too, and Cass figured he was aiming one of those lethal glares at his boss. "It means you're going to put off your plans to befriend Dominic and especially Annette. And you aren't going to help her take my daughter. You're going to come up with some plausible excuse to leave the estate, and then you'll do just that—*leave*."

"And if I don't?"

"I'll tell Dominic who you really are and that you're trying to manipulate his sister." Matt's inflection never changed. He didn't raise his voice. He stayed calm. But he obviously got his point across.

Gideon didn't say a word for several moments, but he did some serious staring at Matt. "You wouldn't do that. Dominic would have me killed if he thought I was working behind his back."

"Yes, he would. And that's the reason you're leaving. Because if I have to choose between you and my daughter, you're going to lose, Gideon."

Cass's phone buzzed. *Great!* What lousy timing. But she had no choice but to answer the call so that the buzzing sound wouldn't alert the trio out front. She expected to hear Hollis's voice.

She didn't.

"It's me, Annette," the caller said.

Cass was so stunned that it took her a moment to respond. She certainly hadn't expected Dominic's sister to contact her. She debated what to say and settled for, "I'm glad you called."

"You might not feel that way when you find out what I want."

Oh, that did sound ominous. "What do you want?" Cass asked cautiously.

"I'd rather not tell you over the phone. That probably wouldn't be a good idea. I want to meet with you, but I don't know if I can trust you. I thought I could trust someone else. Now, I'm not so sure. He's nowhere to be found, and I have to have someone."

Annette was likely talking about Gideon, aka Timothy St. Claire, the man getting a tongue lashing from Matt. And Annette was right to be suspicious of him.

"You can trust me," Cass assured her. "I can help you. What do you need me to do?"

Silence. Well, on Annette's part. Outside, she could

hear Matt still trying to get his point across to Libby, who was pleading with him to go with her.

"Are you and Bill willing to meet with me?" Annette asked.

Were they?

Cass knew there'd be a risk. All right, a *huge* risk. But it was also a chance to get Molly. "I'll meet with you. Just tell me when and where." And she prayed that she wasn't making a fatal mistake.

"Molly's trip home has had a bit of delay. The roads are icy, and even though I'm desperate to see her, I made the driver promise not to rush. So, we have some time. Can you two meet me at the wheelchair ramp at the service entrance of the kitchen at eight o'clock?"

"Sure," Cass said with absolute confidence that she certainly didn't feel.

"Can I really trust you?" Annette asked.

"Yes." Cass knew that wasn't true. She wouldn't do anything to hurt the woman, but one way or another, she did intend to help Matt take Molly. Ultimately, that would betray Annette. It would also get Matt's daughter away from Dominic.

"The real question is—can I trust you?" Cass asked.

But she was talking to herself because Annette had already hung up.

She opened the bathroom door, ready to do whatever battle necessary to get past Gideon and the others, but the only person in the doorway was Matt.

"They're gone?" she whispered. Though a whisper

wasn't necessary. If there was eavesdropping equipment aimed at the cottage, then after the argument Matt had just had, Dominic likely knew he had federal agents or at least suspicious people on the grounds.

"They're gone," Matt verified. She could see that he was still all knotted and riled from the confrontation with Gideon. "But we can't stay here. We'll have to stay in the car. I can move it into the woods—"

"Annette called. She wants us to meet her at the estate. She didn't say why, but she asked for our help."

The tension and anger drained from him, but it was quickly replaced by hope and extreme caution. "When does she want to meet?"

Cass checked her watch. It was 7:45 a.m. "In fifteen minutes." She swallowed hard. "I said yes."

Matt grabbed the jammer, binoculars and the infrared monitor and shoved them into the box of Christmas decoration. Cass knew the box would need to serve as their cover again in case someone stopped them en route to the meeting.

"I'll move the car to the woods before we go," Matt told her. What he didn't add was any speculation about what would happen after that.

"Did I do the right thing by agreeing to this?" Cass whispered.

"We'll know soon enough."

And with that he headed out the door.

Chapter Twelve

Matt had a really bad feeling about this meeting with Annette.

But then, he'd had a bad feeling about their entire plan from the beginning. This was just one more bizarre twist.

"I probably shouldn't have agreed to see Annette, especially in broad daylight," Cass mumbled.

Because they were supposed to meet the woman in less than five minutes, they hurried across the estate lawn, avoiding the shrubs where they'd left the gunman's body. What they couldn't avoid was the brutal wind. No more gray drizzle—yet. Just Arctic blasts from the north. Matt was betting there'd be snow by nightfall. He only hoped it didn't interfere with Molly's rescue.

"Maybe we should have just gone with our original idea of waiting until Molly arrives," Cass added.

"We can still do that." And they might have to. "You do know we aren't just going to go walking up to that kitchen service entrance, right?"

Cass stopped when he did, and they looked at each other. Matt could see the massive concern in her eyes. "It'll be okay," he said, though they both knew that was possibly a lie. "We'll see what Annette wants," he explained. "And then we'll go to the vault to get the security disks."

"How will we get past Annette to do that?"

He shook his head. "I'm not sure yet, but we'll find a way to get inside."

Matt kept the infrared monitor in the box of decorations, but he adjusted it so that it would scan the kitchen service area. The kitchen itself was bustling with activity. He'd expected that, what with the start of Dominic's party less than ten hours from now.

And then he spotted Annette.

He used the binoculars to verify that it was indeed her. Bundled in a thick gray coat that was nearly the same color as the sky, she sat in her wheelchair alone. No sign of Dominic or Gideon. Matt only hoped his boss had heeded his warning and that Libby, Ronald and he were on their way off the estate. He had enough to handle without three federal agents in the mix.

Matt handed Cass the box of decorations. "Keep a close watch on the infrared," he explained. "I don't want anyone ambushing us."

Cass nodded, came up on her tiptoes and gave him a quick kiss. "For luck," she said.

Matt hoped they didn't need it. He also hoped he was wrong about the kiss. It didn't feel as if it was only for luck. It felt as intimate as it could get. But then, a lot of things felt intimate with Cass.

He pushed that uneasy feeling aside, and they walked toward Annette. The woman lifted her hand when she spotted them. Her reaction looked innocent enough, and she seemed genuinely pleased to see them.

But appearances could be deceiving.

"I wasn't sure you'd come," Annette said. "I'm thankful you did." She looked around them while the wind whipped at her dark shoulder-length hair. "We should talk out here, because I don't want Dominic to hear us. He has eavesdropping devices in parts of the house."

"What happened, Annette?" Cass asked.

"Too much. I had a friend who was going to help me, but when he showed up and I was able to meet him in person for the first time, I wasn't sure I could trust him. Truth is, he might even be working for my brother."

Matt was afraid of the same thing.

She glanced at both of them. "My brother has a new business partner, and he'll be arriving tonight for the party. Dominic wouldn't do anything to physically hurt Molly or me, but I believe this man would. I had him checked out, and he actually kidnapped his former partner's son and forced the boy's father to hand over some money that was in dispute. The man is dangerous, and I don't want him to get the opportunity to kidnap Molly."

Matt didn't doubt that about Sylvester Marquez, and if all went well with Molly's rescue, he made a mental note to do more checking into this guy.

"I've tried to talk to my brother about this," Annette continued. "He won't listen. He says he can keep his new partner under control, that I should trust him. Well, I might trust Dominic on most things, but I can't turn a blind eye while he brings that man into our lives."

"How can we help?" Matt asked. He glanced at the infrared monitor to make sure they were still alone. They were.

Annette paused, and her forehead bunched up. "I'm taking a huge risk just by telling you these things. And I'm going to take an even bigger risk with what I'm about to ask you to do. I want you to help me get Molly away from the estate."

Other than the howl of the wind, everything went silent. Matt's heart started to pound. This could be the answer to some prayers.

Or the start of a deadly nightmare.

"You're positive your brother has no idea you're planning this?" Matt asked.

Annette shook her head. "He doesn't know."

Matt hoped like hell that was true, but the reality was that Dominic might indeed be aware of it.

"I want to leave with Molly tonight while the party is going on," Annette continued. Her lips were trembling now, and he suspected the rest of her was, too. "I've arranged for a car to be waiting out back, but I can't get her out of the house by myself. Nor can I drive. And I can't risk using the chauffeur because he's loyal to my brother."

Matt had so many questions, but one topped the list. "Who helped you arrange for the car?"

She shook her head. "I'd rather not tell you. But he knows you. I talked to him about you last night, and he says I can trust you."

It was no doubt Hollis. At least, he hoped it was Hollis rather than Gideon, even though Matt didn't trust either of them.

Of course, the car was a moot point. He didn't plan on helping Annette steal his child.

"Since you work here, you can already get into the estate, of course," Annette continued. "But I can give you access codes to bypass the security system just in case you have to enter or exit through a monitored door. I can also show you where you can hide until it's time for you to leave."

"Hide?" Cass asked. Matt had the same question.

"There's a panic room off the nursery. It's exactly like the one Dominic has in his office. I had it added for security reasons, in case someone broke into the estate. I wanted a safe place to hide with Molly. There's an underground tunnel that leads from the panic room outside. And that's where the car will be waiting."

Cass lifted an eyebrow and silently asked him— what do we do now?

Matt wasn't sure. He couldn't tell Annette no. If he

did, she might think he would go to Dominic and rat her out. Or she might beef up security to the point that they'd never get inside.

"I'll pay you well," Annette added.

Matt pretended to think about it before he nodded. "We'll help."

She flattened her hand on her chest, and it seemed as if the anxiety and fear drained from her body. "Thank God—you're the answer to my prayers. Now, let's get in out of this weather before we all catch pneumonia." She took a slip of paper from her coat pocket and handed it to Matt. "Those are the security codes to get into the house. Come at exactly 8:00 p.m. and go into the nursery panic room. Wait there until I can get away from the party."

"What about the guards and the nanny?" Cass asked.

"I'll tell the guards they won't be needed in the nursery area. As for the nanny, I plan to slip her some of my sleeping pills. I know, that sounds terrible, but she's also very loyal to Dominic, and I can't risk her trying to stop us. Now, come with me so I can show you where you'll need to hide. But once we're inside, please don't mention any of this."

Even though they obviously weren't going to carry on a sensitive conversation and even though they were being escorted into the house by Annette, Matt didn't take any chances. Once Annette was ahead of them and unable to see what he was doing, he reached in the box and pressed the jammer. He didn't want Cass's face and his showing up on any of the surveillance disks.

"This way," Annette instructed, leading them through the servants' entrance.

They passed at least a half-dozen workers, all of whom never gave them a second glance. Then Annette led them through the maze of hallways.

Cass cleared her throat, garnering his attention, and she pointed to the infrared thermal blobs that were headed their way. A moment later Matt heard the voices associated with those blobs.

Two men.

"It's Dominic," Cass frantically whispered.

Ahead of them Annette didn't have a panicked reaction. She kept on moving her motorized wheel-chair toward the nursery. Judging from the sound of the voices, the men were close. Too close. And if Cass and he turned and ran, it might alarm Annette to the point that she would send guards after them. But they couldn't just come face-to-face with Dominic, either, because he would recognize Cass.

And he would almost certainly try to kill her.

Matt caught onto Cass's arm and shoved her into a bedroom just as Dominic and Hollis rounded the corner. Both men stopped. A surprised and concerned Hollis nailed his attention to Matt, but Dominic's gaze landed on his sister.

"You were outside," he said to Annette, obviously noting the coat and her wind-reddened face. "You shouldn't have been. You'll catch your death from cold."

And with that ominous warning still on his lips,

Dominic walked closer and turned that scrutinizing gaze on Matt.

The departmental reports about him had been accurate. Dominic was six-foot-three, with black hair and piercing amber-brown eyes. What the reports hadn't said was that the man had a formidable presence. But then that didn't surprise Matt. Dominic was as powerful as he was lethal.

What did surprise him was his gut reaction to the man. He despised him, yes, because for all practical purposes, Dominic had stolen his daughter. But Matt had another reaction to him, too. He was jealous. Not the sentiment Matt wanted to feel, but it was there.

Cass had obviously been attracted to this man.

And jealousy was a dangerous emotion that had no place in this rescue mission. It only confirmed his fears that his feelings for Cass were making him lose focus.

He couldn't do that, not with so much at stake.

Matt didn't dare check over his shoulder to make sure that Cass was hidden away. He knew she would be. His bigger concern right now was that Annette would notice Cass missing and ask where she was. Cass and he didn't need questions, nor did they need to deal with what Dominic's response would be. Matt needed to make this impromptu meeting fast and hopefully painless.

"You are?" Dominic demanded.

"Bill," Annette calmly provided. "I want some Christmas decorations in the nursery, and he's going to help. Hollis, you don't mind if I borrow him for a while, do you?"

For a petite, wheelchair-bound woman, she had some authority in her voice, and she practically dared Hollis to object to her *request*. Annette had backbone, and that concerned Matt. Because she certainly hadn't shown that backbone in situations with her brother.

So, was her weakness all an act?

Dominic took another step toward Matt, and he met him eye-to-eye. It was a war of sorts. Dominic was likely waiting for him to cower or look submissive. Matt tried to do his best, for the sake of ending this encounter, but he was certain that he failed. He wasn't the cowering or submissive type.

"Do your job fast," Dominic warned. "I don't want you in the house any longer than absolutely necessary."

Matt stepped to the side so that Hollis and Dominic could get by. He also blocked the doorway of the bedroom just in case one of the men looked in and spotted Cass.

"This way," Annette said once the men were out of sight and earshot.

Cass peeked out of the room, checking to make sure it was safe before she came out and fell in step alongside Matt. "Close call," she mouthed.

Oh, yeah.

It might be days before his stomach unknotted.

Annette led them into the nursery. She didn't comment at all about what had just happened. Instead, she moved in her wheelchair to the right wall. There was no sign of a panic room door and no decorative object that could have hidden the mechanism to open it.

So, was this some sort of trick?

Matt checked the infrared to make sure they weren't about to be attacked in a trap of Annette's making.

But Annette meandered around the room as if looking for the right place to add those holiday decorations. She touched her index finger to the corner, about three feet from the floor. And the wall began to slide apart.

"Oops, I didn't mean to do that," she said, no doubt for the sake of anyone listening. "My brother and I have these rooms for security purposes. I'm sure you understand."

Matt caught just a glimpse of the panic room on the other side before she tapped the spot again, and it closed.

"You know, I don't think I want this room decorated after all," Annette said as she pretended to study the walls. "Molly is just at the right age to grab things she shouldn't. I'm really sorry to have brought you all the way in here for nothing."

"No problem," Matt insisted. "If you change your mind, just let us know."

Annette nodded. "Eight o'clock," she whispered.

Matt returned the nod, and Cass and he got out of there. Once they were away from Annette, he checked the infrared and saw they had a clear path to the end of the hall.

But not to the vault.

They had to take a detour to avoid the trio of figures near the kitchen. Matt couldn't take the chance that one of those figures might be Dominic.

"You think Annette is leading us into a trap?" Cass whispered.

"It's possible, but we knew she was planning on trying to escape with Molly. Maybe she's more desperate than we thought."

At least, that's what Matt hoped, because he didn't care for the alternative.

They hurried through the halls and down the stairs that led to the vault.

"I won't be long," Cass mumbled, handing him the box.

She used Hollis's codes again to open the vault, and she went inside. Matt stood watch and kept his attention on the infrared. But he'd barely begun his watch duty when he heard Cass curse.

"What's wrong now?"

When she didn't answer, he glanced inside to see what'd prompted her response. It didn't take Matt long to figure it out.

The shelf had a large gap where some of the surveillance disks were missing. But they weren't just any disks.

No.

They were the very ones that Cass needed to prove her innocence.

CASS'S HEART FELT as if someone had closed a tight fist around it. Those disks had been her lifeline, her hope to clearing her name.

Now they were gone.

And the hope was gone, as well.

But that feeling of hopelessness was quickly replaced by another. One of grave concern. Why had the disks been removed?

Had Dominic gotten suspicious?

"We need to get out of here," Matt ordered. And he obviously had the same thought as she had. Perhaps Annette wasn't the trap.

Maybe this was.

Maybe Dominic had somehow figured out that she was there at the estate, and he'd set up this elaborate game to punish her. He might let her think she was close to getting her freedom, only to snatch it away from her.

But Cass couldn't let that possibility stop her.

She grabbed the box of decorations from Matt so that his hands would be free to get to his weapon, and she checked the infrared. No one was lurking at the stairs waiting for them, but with all the movement in the house, it was impossible to tell if someone had found a way to monitor them.

They hurried into the hall and headed for the servants' entrance so they could go out the same way they came in.

Cass's concerns skyrocketed when they reached the top of the stairs and she heard the voices. And on the infrared, she saw the group of people approaching. Matt immediately pulled her into the doorway of one of the rooms. Probably in case Dominic was about to make a return visit.

But it wasn't Dominic.

Cass didn't recognize the woman's voice, but she did recognize the tiny sound she heard. It was a baby making fussy noises.

"Molly," Matt whispered.

And in his voice she could hear all the emotions that he'd been fighting to keep under control. But it would be next to impossible not to react to the fact that his daughter was only a few yards away.

He stepped out of the doorway before Cass could figure out if she should stop him. After all, they did have permission to be in the house, and Annette would likely vouch for them if there were questions. Plus, there was that whole part about her not being able to stop him. Judging from his intense expression, he was going to see his daughter.

Cass peeked out so she could cover his back in case this situation took a turn for the worse. However, it all seemed routine. Almost mundane. The tall formidable-looking blond nanny had Molly in a stroller, and she was pushing the child toward the nursery. Molly was squirming, tugging at the lap strap that held her firmly in place, and she was babbling sounds of protest.

The nanny stopped cold, probably because Matt was blocking her path to the nursery. "Can I help you?" the woman asked, but her tone was more like a bark from him to get out of her way.

Molly continued to fuss.

Matt continued to stand there and stare at his baby.

And Cass knew she had to do something or the nanny just might shout out for the guards or Dominic.

"My, my," Cass said, stepping out. She leaned down so she could make eye contact with Molly. "Are you sleepy, sweetheart?" she asked the baby.

Molly stared at her with those suspicious blue eyes—Matt's eyes—and she volleyed glances between Cass and him.

"She didn't sleep well last night," the nanny explained. "Nor did I. We both need naps." She gripped the stroller handles and proceeded to move forward.

Matt didn't back up.

He seemed frozen, unable to take his eyes off his child. Cass couldn't blame him. It was amazing. Father and daughter seeing each other for the first time.

But this visit had to end.

"Bill," Cass said, remembering to use his fake name.

The fake name had hardly left her mouth when the armed guard rounded the corner. He, too, stopped and eyed them.

"Is there a problem?" he called out to the nanny.

"No," Cass quickly assured him.

She caught Matt's arm and pulled him aside so the nanny could get by. And that's exactly what she did. However, the guard stayed in place and stared at them.

"We're putting up decorations for Annette," Cass volunteered.

With a now precarious hold on both Matt and the box, Cass got him moving toward the servants' entrance.

"I want to get her out of here now," Matt mumbled. It seemed as if he had to fight to utter each word.

"I know. But we can't. It's safer and smarter if we stick with the plan."

That seemed to do the trick, and he sped up his steps. Unfortunately, they had to slow down again when Cass heard a voice she didn't want to hear.

Dominic.

Mercy, what else was going to go wrong?

He was in the doorway of the servants' entrance. Talking to Hollis.

Matt and she ducked into the butler's pantry before either Hollis or Dominic could see them. Cass wasn't sure her heart could withstand too much more of this emotional roller-coaster ride, what with Annette's offer, the missing security disks, Matt seeing his baby for the first time and now a second near encounter with Dominic.

"What was my sister doing out in the cold?" she heard Dominic ask Hollis.

And Cass was extremely interested in what her informant had to say. She peeked out at them.

"Said she needed fresh air," Hollis answered. All in all, it was a good, deceptive answer.

One that Dominic apparently didn't like.

"You have orders to bring her back in if you see her outside. I want her monitored at all times. I've already told you that she's losing her grip on reality."

That was BS. It was Dominic who was losing control of his sister. He obviously didn't like that.

"What about the guy Annette has putting up Christmas decorations," Dominic continued. "You trust him?"

"I don't know anything about him."

It was another jolt for Cass. That wasn't an answer she wanted to hear, and judging from the way Matt cursed under his breath, neither did he.

"Come on, Hollis," Dominic prompted. "You make a point of knowing everything about everyone."

"Not this time. He sorta dropped out of nowhere. Suspicious, if you ask me."

"Is that some sort of warning?"

"Take it for what it is," Hollis answered.

Cass suddenly wanted to throttle her well-paid informant. She didn't know if Hollis was just being sly, or if he truly wanted Dominic to be suspicious of them.

"You might want to check into your sister's pen pal, too," Hollis advised. "There's something not right about that guy."

"I have that matter under control," Dominic said.

It sounded ominous. And probably was. But what did it mean? Was Dominic aware that Gideon was a federal agent? Or was Gideon on Dominic's payroll?

"Find Annette's Christmas *decorator*," Dominic ordered Hollis. "Keep a close watch on him. And post guards in every hall. I don't want anyone else wandering around here."

"Will do," Hollis said, and he strolled away.

But Dominic didn't move. He stayed put, and he looked outside as if watching for someone. Hopefully, he wouldn't stay there long, because every second that passed was a second that someone might spot them, and they would have to explain what they were doing in the butler's pantry.

"I'm sorry you couldn't take Molly," Cass whispered.

"Me, too. But the extra guards won't stop me. She's leaving this place with us tonight."

Yes, but first they had to get past Dominic and regroup. They also needed a backup plan, several of them, and somehow Cass had to come to terms with the fact that Dominic had likely destroyed the disks—the very thing she needed to prove her innocence.

"There you are," Dominic said.

Cass's heart jolted, until she realized he wasn't speaking to them but rather someone who'd just come through the service entrance.

"I trust you had a pleasant morning walk," Dominic added.

"Yes." It was a woman's voice. She stepped into the room, bringing the cold and some fresh snow-flakes with her.

Cass's heart jolted again. When she saw the visitor.

It was Special Agent Libby Rayburn.

Libby stepped into Dominic's arms as if she belonged there, and she kissed him.

Chapter Thirteen

"Libby," Matt snarled under his breath.

And he checked his watch—again. By God, he should have had answers by now.

He'd been snarling his fellow agent's name all day, since he'd seen her in a lip-lock with Dominic. What the hell was going on? Better yet, would Libby's presence and that kiss impact the rescue mission that was only two hours away?

"The minutes aren't going to pass any faster if you keep checking the time," Cass remarked.

But Matt couldn't help himself. In two hours he could have his daughter. In two hours and twenty minutes, they could be off the estate.

If things went as planned.

The plan was to use the jammer one last time to enter the estate. Not at eight o'clock as Annette had insisted. But as soon as it got dark, which should happen around 6:00 p.m. since the iron-gray sky and the snow were practically shutting out the sun.

Once inside the estate, Matt would incapacitate anyone who might try to stop him as he took Molly. Then he'd hurry back to the car that Matt had hidden in the woods just beyond the cottage.

The car where Cass and he had spent most of the day.

Talking.

Freezing.

And keeping watch on the estate with the infrared and binoculars.

Matt had covered the car as best he could with fallen tree limbs, and the snow had given them a good half inch dusting. They weren't totally concealed, but a person would have to look hard to find them. So far, no one had come close to looking, and Matt didn't think they would. All the activity was centered on the house with everyone getting ready for the big Christmas Eve party. Hopefully, that party would be the perfect cover for a quick, quiet rescue.

Beside him on the car seat, Cass gave their single blanket another adjustment. She tried to cover both of them, something Matt had insisted she not do. He wanted her to take the full blanket. But she'd refused, of course, and was trying to keep them both warm.

Cass was right next to him, practically in his lap. On one hand, Matt welcomed the shared body heat. On the other, he didn't welcome the distraction that the body heat was creating.

The dangerous energy boiling inside didn't help.

He wanted to do something. *Anything.* He wanted to move. But he couldn't. They needed to stay put so they wouldn't risk being seen.

Matt's phone vibrated, and he immediately checked the screen. "Ronald," he snapped, answering it. "I've waited all day for a call from you."

"I know, and I'm sorry. I got your message about Libby still being at the estate, and I've been trying to figure out what's going on."

"And?"

"I don't have much. Gideon or someone has hidden Dominic's files. The department might be using Libby to try to gain Dominic's cooperation so she can get information that'll either lead to his arrest or the arrest of his new business associate."

"She kissed Dominic," Matt informed him. "I saw it with my own eyes. They aren't just chummy, Ronald. Something's going on."

"Maybe. Or else maybe her assignment is to gain Dominic's cooperation any way she can." He paused. "Still, if she kissed him, then it would appear that she's been at this relationship or assignment for a while. It certainly wasn't something she mentioned to me."

"Nor me."

"I did find out something interesting about Annette Cordova, though. Did you know she's been in contact with Collena Drake?"

Matt knew the name. From what Cass had told him, Collena Drake was a former cop at SAPD, and she was now heading the task force to locate all the illegally adopted babies. Collena had apparently been digging through the hundreds of files left by the criminals at the now infamous Brighton Birthing Centre where the illegal adoptions had originated. But piecing together the information was like a huge puzzle, and to make the process easier, she'd been posting information on a public website in addition to asking the public for help.

Matt didn't like the immediate conclusion that came to mind. "Does Annette know that I'm Molly's father?"

"She does if she can put two and two together. Collena knew the identity of the baby's birth mother, and all Annette had to do was figure out who Vanessa's lover was fifteen months ago."

That wasn't a stretch, since it was exactly the way Cass had learned that he was Molly's father. And since Vanessa and he hadn't exactly kept their relationship a secret. Heck, their picture had even ended up in the newspaper when he escorted her to a fancy charity ball.

Of course, this made Matt even more suspicious of Annette.

"Where are you?" Matt asked.

"In a blink-and-miss-it-size town about thirty minutes from the estate. I decided to stay close if you needed me. And in case you missed it, Matt, I'm offering to help you in any way I can."

Matt really wanted to accept Ronald's help, but he wasn't sure he could trust him. In fact, he wasn't sure he should have trusted Ronald with the bit of information he'd just told him about Libby. Ronald could know every detail about what Libby was doing. Heck, he could even be the one responsible for the leak in communication since the main suspects for that leak were Libby, Ronald and Gideon.

Trusting anyone now was too big a risk.

"I wish you'd give up this dangerous attempt to get your baby," Ronald told him.

"I have," Matt lied. "I'm driving back to San Antonio. I've decided to go through official channels to get Molly away from Dominic."

Silence for several moments. "What about Cass— is she with you?" Ronald asked.

"She left earlier," Matt lied again. Why, he didn't know exactly, but he didn't think it was a good idea for Ronald to know too much.

Cass gave him a questioning glance but then nodded. She obviously didn't want him to tell Ronald the truth, either. So, Matt decided to go with a few more lies. If Ronald was a snitch, or a traitor, then a lie or two might send him and anyone else who was listening off on a wild goose chase.

"Cass found the evidence to exonerate her," Matt explained.

"Oh. I see." Ronald cleared his throat. "Well, she should have brought it straight to me."

"She doesn't trust you, Gideon, Libby or anyone else in the department. Including me."

More silence. "So, what's she going to do?"

"I'm not sure, but with her old contacts, she'll find someone who can get the evidence into the right hands, or maybe even the press."

"You think she'll go to the newspapers?" Was it Matt's imagination that Ronald was highly concerned about that?

"That's what I would do. Then the press can start asking questions and digging for the truth." And Matt left it at that. "Ronald, if you hear anything about Libby, call me."

"That was clever," Cass commented when he ended the call. "You think Ronald believes you?"

Matt shrugged. "Hard to tell. But it might make Gideon, Libby and him leave the estate to look for you. I'd rather them be anywhere but here."

"True. What about Libby? Did Ronald have a theory for that?"

"She might be trying to worm her way into Dominic's trust and heart."

"Hmmph. Unless she's got a huge bank account, that won't happen. Still, I suppose she could be playing the part of a wealthy prospect."

"Or she could have sold out to Dominic," he pointed out.

Cass bobbed her head. "Ronald or Gideon could have done the same. In fact, you could possibly be the only honest agent within a hundred miles of here."

Now he smiled. Matt wasn't sure how she could keep up her spirits under the circumstances, but Cass was managing it. "Have I said I'm sorry that you couldn't find the surveillance disks?"

"About a dozen times, but it's nice to hear it again." She pulled in her breath. "I really thought this would work, that I'd be able to find the proof I needed. Now I'll need to come up with a different plan."

"Yet, here you are helping me." He turned toward her and adjusted the blanket so that she'd be covered. "It wasn't supposed to work this way."

She made a sound of dismissal. "Right now there's nothing more important than getting your daughter."

"You really mean that." And it wasn't a question. "Now we both might have to live on the run."

The corner of her mouth lifted. "Misery loves company," she mumbled. Then the smile faded. "But that life isn't for Molly and you."

"We might not have a choice. I'm breaking the law every time I go onto Dominic's property."

"Technically. But you could also say that you're in pursuit of a felon. And we haven't exactly broken in. We've walked in through unlocked doors or entered at Annette's invitation. Plus, Dominic illegally adopted Molly, and that means you have every right to claim her."

"Through legal channels, yes." The blanket slipped off her, and Cass and he bumped hands trying to reposition it.

"You'll get around to those legal channels, but as you know, we can't trust them right now."

It made Matt wonder. What would happen after tonight? Would Cass just leave and try to come up with another plan to gain her freedom?

"The snow is pretty," she said, looking through the branches and the few bare spots on the windshield. "A white Christmas. I haven't had one of those in years."

He had. White Christmases in places where he was undercover. Places where being single at Christmas didn't matter because he had no one to go home to.

No family.

No significant other.

But it would matter now. And that brought him back to the same question that'd been going through his mind.

"What'll happen after tonight?" he asked aloud, something he hadn't planned.

"Your life will change forever." Cass made it sound as if she'd given it lots of thought. And she probably had. "Nothing will ever be the same again. Oh, and you'll have to learn to change diapers and talk baby talk."

She looked up. Smiled. Man, it was dazzling. She probably didn't know a smile could light up her entire face. And for some reason that smile caught Matt right in the heart. He was getting a new life with his daughter, and Cass was getting nothing.

"Don't look sad." She reached out and touched her index finger to his lips.

He caught her hand before she could pull it away.

"Man, you're really freezing. I can turn on the engine and the heat—"

"No." And she grabbed his hand when he reached for the keys. "We've already been through this. Someone might see the exhaust and come to investigate. We don't need that, not when we're this close to getting Molly."

Still, he could do something to warm her. He pulled her even nearer to him. She cooperated, probably because she needed the heat to keep from going numb. She not only snuggled, Cass put her face against his neck.

His mind immediately registered that there was a problem being this close to Cass. After all, they'd had zero success in resisting each other—especially when under stress.

But he couldn't let her freeze, either, and his brain seemed perfectly content with offering that kind of comfort. Too bad his body took that contentment a step further. Parts of him stirred at the contact.

"I hope the roads won't be slick tonight," Matt mumbled. "I don't want anything to slow down the escape."

While he had his mind on the plan, he checked the infrared monitor. There were still people milling all around the estate. Annette was in the nursery with Molly. Dominic or someone of his body size was in his office. Libby had either left the estate, or she was one of the heat blobs in one of the many guest rooms. And there were more people arriving.

In other words, nothing had changed in the past hours.

"Want to hear something I've never told anyone?" Cass asked. Her breath was warm, the only warm thing in the car, and it hit against his neck. He welcomed it, though it stirred yet more warmth in his body.

"Sure." Anything to pass the time. And anything to get his mind off her. Except, he couldn't seem to do that.

He kept looking at her, at the hair that she'd pushed almost haphazardly away from her ivory face. At her eyes—the color of a Christmas tree. At her mouth. No lipstick for her, but her mouth was still the color of some exotic flower.

Hell.

Christmas-tree eyes, exotic-flower lips, an ivory face? Oh, man. These were not descriptions normally in his vocabulary.

Green eyes. Pink lips. Pale face.

There.

That was better.

"My dad was a thief," she confessed, obviously unaware of the mental battle he was having with himself. "He used to infiltrate companies and steal secrets. He made a fortune and was eventually arrested. The Justice Department then hired him as a consultant. That's how I met Gideon. Before my parents were killed in a car accident two years ago, Gideon was Dad's supervisor of sorts."

Matt shook his head. "I had no idea."

And he still couldn't get his mind off her lips.

"It was all kept pretty hush-hush." She looked up at him. This time, her breath brushed his face. Like a kiss. "So, you see, I'm not really a debutante heiress. I'm just a woman who inherited her father's ill-gotten gains. Sometimes I think that's why fate is doing a number on me."

Without thinking, Matt traced the bruise on her cheek with his fingertips. "You don't deserve what fate's done to you," he assured her.

And they both froze.

Cass stared at him. He stared at her. And she finally shook her head. "That sounded—"

"Sappy," he finished. "Like Christmas-tree eyes and exotic-flower lips."

"Well, I was going to say it sounded *scary*. And then I was going to add that fate hasn't been so kind to you, either." She stared at him, frowned. "'Exotic-flower lips?' Care to explain that one?"

"Not in a million years."

Her frown curved into a slow, sly smile. "If it's any consolation—I was thinking that your eyes are the color of a Ulysses butterfly. Butterfly blue."

That should have made him groan. "Butterfly blue? Poetic."

"Yes." Her smile went south. "But how did this happen? How did we end up feeling…*poetic* about each other?"

Since she made it seem a little like a death sentence, Matt couldn't help it. He chuckled. "Temporary insanity. We're in a highly dangerous situation. Our bodies are probably…"

Now, it was his turn to pause. Good grief. He'd talked himself into a corner. There was nowhere to go with that comment. Well, nowhere that wouldn't get him in trouble.

"Attraction is a funny thing," she concluded.

"*Funny* isn't the word I'd use. *Uncomfortable,* maybe."

"Yes." Cass agreed. "Uncomfortable. Poetic, even. Maybe even stupid. But at least I'm a little warmer now."

Oh, yeah. Warmer. Crazier. And obsessed with the woman whose breast and elbow brushed his ribs.

Every logical thought he had in his head told him to look away from her and do something official—like keep watching the estate. But that little voice in the back of his head kept telling him that his butterfly-blue eyes wanted to look at her Christmas-tree-green ones.

"Exotic-flower lips," he muttered.

And that's when he really lost it. One look at those eyes, those lips, that face, and he lowered his head and kissed her.

Part of him, the logical part, hoped that Cass would slap him or something. But she slid her arms around his neck and returned the kiss.

He was in major trouble here.

But that didn't stop him. Nothing short of Cass saying no would stop him. She was warm, welcoming and inviting, and he wanted to taste those lips. He wanted to feel her body against his.

Heck, he just wanted *her*.

He slid his hand beneath her shirt, warming it first on her stomach, before cupping her right breast. No bra. Which meant there were no obstacles to touching her. So that's what he did, and he savored every breathy moan of pleasure that she made until it wasn't enough for either of them.

Matt used his mouth then.

He slid down in the seat, lifted her top and tasted the nipples that'd been driving him crazy since the moment he met her.

"You taste expensive," he teased. Though he didn't feel like teasing her. The need was already overtaking him. His body was already begging.

She lay back on the seat, making it easier for him to continue his kisses. Cass pressed against him, arching her hips. Seeking him.

Matt accommodated her. He lowered himself, trying to keep his weight off her, but Cass would have no part of that. She pulled him on top of her, weight and all, and hooked her legs around the backs of his. In the process she banged her knee on the steering wheel, a reminder that the logistics of car sex was best left to teenagers and fools.

They obviously fell into the latter category.

Still, that didn't stop him from escalating the kisses. He touched her, sliding his hand down her stomach and into the waist of her loose jeans. But this time the touching didn't last long. She put her hands between them and unzipped him.

And then she touched him in exactly the right place. Matt lost his breath for a few seconds, but he didn't let that stop him from returning the favor. He unzipped her and slipped her jeans off her legs. He touched. And kissed. And fueled the fire in both of them until they both needed more.

The kisses and touches became hotter. Faster. Everything became faster. His breathing. His heartbeat. His pulse. Thoughts raced through his head, but there was really only one primal thought that he could latch on to. *Take her.*

Cass's fingers dug into his back, and she fought to bring him closer, to make the kisses deeper. Her sounds of yearning and need quickly turned to frantic desperation. Matt understood both, because his own body was making the same demands.

The seat was their enemy, but logistics and discomfort weren't going to stop the heat that was racing out of control.

Her scent was all around her. Mercy, that scent. All woman. All need.

"Take me."

Matt wasn't sure if she said the words aloud or if she said them silently with the hungry look in her eyes. But it didn't matter. It was time he did something about this primal need raging through them.

He fumbled in the equipment bag, took out a condom and put it on. Cass didn't wait even a second before she took him and guided him inside her.

Matt shook his head, to clear it, to try to adjust to the pleasure that was overwhelming him. But it was useless. The need took over. As it always would. And Matt found the rhythm that would end all of this too soon.

"Take me," Cass repeated, her voice all heat and silk.

Matt pulled back slightly so he could see her face. The heat and silk were there, too. As was the urgency.

She used her legs to tighten her grip on him. Her hands went into his hair to pull him closer. They moved as one, in a frantic race to find some kind of relief to the unbearable need.

When he felt her shudder, and her body closed around his, Matt gathered her close, kissed her and let himself fall.

CASS WAS WARM NOW.

Too bad it wouldn't last.

The moment Matt pulled away from her, she felt the loss.

Not just of his body heat. The loss of *him*.

With the sun sinking low on the horizon, their quiet together time was almost over. They'd soon go into the estate, where any and everything could happen. But she refused to think about that now. She allowed herself to settle into his arms, and for the next few minutes she pretended that all was right with the world. There were no men like Dominic. No illegal adoptions. Just Matt and Molly living the life they deserved.

And her, of course.

Except Cass didn't know where she fit in. Without the security disks or any other concrete evidence, she didn't have a ticket to freedom. Matt would get that ticket. She was sure of it. The department wouldn't toss a father in jail for rescuing his child.

But the Justice Department probably wouldn't extend that courtesy to her. If she couldn't get away after the rescue, if she was caught, she'd go to jail.

Oh, Matt would do his best to get her out, but justice wouldn't be on her side. Because the Justice Department needed Dominic, and they would do whatever it took to maintain a relationship with him. In the grand scheme of things, she was expendable so that the feds could ultimately arrest some dangerous criminals that Dominic was apparently willing to hand over to them.

If she went to jail, Dominic would find a way to kill her. Cass didn't doubt that. And it wasn't fair or reasonable to ask Matt to spend his life protecting her.

She'd have to go on the run again.

Far away from Matt and Molly so that she wouldn't drag them into the chaos of her life. Even though she'd only seen Molly a few precious moments, Cass wanted only the very best for the little girl.

And for Matt.

That meant she couldn't be part of his life.

Just the thought of it sent an almost unbearable ache through her. She tried to convince herself that it was caused by the temporary closeness brought on by sex and intense physical attraction.

But she wasn't that good a liar.

Just like Molly, Matt was important to her, and Cass wondered if she'd spend the rest of her life aching for them, for the man and the family that she could never have.

She felt a hot tear slide down her cheek, and she swiped it away before Matt could notice. Cass didn't want him to think she regretted what'd happened. She didn't. But it hurt to know this was the one and only time she'd make love with him.

"I want you to stay here," Matt said, "while I go into the estate."

"No." Cass didn't even have to think about it. She moved so she could make eye contact with him. So he could see the determination in her eyes. This was not negotiable. "You'll need backup. You need my help, and you're going to get it whether you want it or not."

"Oh, I want it," he admitted. "I can't risk anything but success tonight. But I also can't risk you getting hurt when you don't have a stake in this."

She had a stake all right—Matt and Molly's safety.

Cass gave him a quick peck on the cheek. "No more talk about me staying here. We do this together."

He stayed quiet a moment and then pointed to the infrared monitor that they'd put on the dash. "Molly's alone in the nursery."

She was. Well, almost. There was someone just outside the nursery door. But the good news was that Molly appeared to be in her crib, and since she wasn't moving around, she was likely asleep.

"It's time to leave," Matt whispered, moving even farther away from her so he could adjust his clothes.

Cass had just watched the last of the light leave the sky. She felt her hopes for her own future go right along with it.

She sat up and put her clothes back on. Matt didn't take the box of decorations from the back seat. Instead, he grabbed his equipment bag and put both the jammer and the infrared monitor in it.

"We're not going to use the decorations as our cover?" she asked.

He shook his head. "If anyone stops me, I'll just say Annette asked me to do some minor repairs for her. And I'll tell them I have my tools in this equipment bag."

Cass nodded and tested the size of her coat pocket. Some of the equipment would fit, but she would also need easy access to her gun.

Which brought her full circle to what she'd been thinking about. "If something goes wrong—"

"You're not going," Matt interrupted.

Before Cass could huff and reiterate that she was indeed going, she felt the cold metal slap across her left wrist. One click. Immediately followed by another.

And she realized, too late, that Matt had handcuffed her to the steering wheel.

"What do you think you're doing?" Cass practically howled.

"Saving your life."

With that, he shut the car door, looped the equipment bag over his shoulder and raced toward the estate.

Chapter Fourteen

Matt didn't look back.

With the darkness and the snow, he wouldn't be able to see Cass anyway. Besides, he didn't have to see her to know that she was mad enough to spit nails. For reasons he didn't want to explore right now, Cass seemed willing to risk her life for this rescue.

On one level, he desperately wanted her help. But if something went wrong, if she got hurt or worse, he wouldn't be able to live with that. He only hoped he could do this rescue quietly and without alerting anyone inside the house.

It definitely wasn't the best weather for a rescue mission. It was bitter cold, and the snow was coming down hard now. There was probably only an hour or so at most where the roads would still be passable.

Matt went to the service entrance where Cass and he had met with Annette earlier. This would be his entry route, but on the way out, he'd go through the garden room that had been empty most of the day.

Hopefully, it would stay that way.

He glanced down into the equipment bag and saw all the warm bodies displayed on infrared. He couldn't do much about that. Maybe he could blend in. Still, he hit the jammer to disrupt the security system so that no one would be able to monitor him with the surveillance cameras.

He walked into the massive kitchen as if he had every right to be there. No one, including an armed guard who was sampling the party food, even looked his way. Matt took full advantage of that and proceeded through the butler's pantry, but he stopped when he heard voices in the hall.

Voices that he recognized.

Ronald and Libby.

What the hell was Ronald doing here? And why did his fellow agents keep showing up at the worst possible moments?

Matt could only hear snatches of their conversation. Even though they were practically whispering, it was clear they were arguing.

"Leaving now would be a mistake," Libby insisted. "I'm close to getting what the department wants."

"You're close to getting yourself killed," Ronald snarled.

"This isn't personal for me like it is for Matt," Libby countered.

"That may be, but Matt had the good sense to leave."

So, his lie had worked after all. That surprised him

a little, and Matt wondered why Libby, Ronald or even Gideon hadn't scanned the grounds with infrared to find him. Maybe they'd taken him at his word that Cass and he had both left the estate.

Matt debated if he should step out and confront them. But he couldn't trust them, and he didn't have to time to do anything but rescue Molly. So, the moment they rounded the corner, he made his way toward the nursery.

He took out a pistol-size stun gun and carried it in his left hand just in case he had to go for his Glock. That would be a last resort, of course, because he couldn't fire. He couldn't risk hitting Molly.

The bored-looking guard that Matt had seen on infrared was still positioned outside the nursery door. Matt didn't slow his stride. He didn't make eye contact with the man. But as soon as he was within reaching distance, he popped the guy's neck with the stun gun. The guard didn't have time to react. He went down like a sack of rocks.

Matt didn't waste any time. He grabbed the guard by the back of his collar, opened the nursery door and dragged him inside to the other side of the sofa.

He hurried to the crib where Molly was indeed sleeping. She was on her side, tucked beneath a thick pink blanket.

Just the sight of her nearly brought him to his knees.

Even though he'd only known about his daughter for a few days, the love he felt for her was overwhelming, and he had to force himself not to stand there and just look at her. There'd be plenty of time for that later.

He shoved the stun gun into his pocket and reached for her.

He'd never held a baby before. He prayed he wasn't so clumsy and bumbling that he woke her. He really needed her to stay asleep so he could try to get her out through the garden room.

Matt eased his hand beneath her head, beneath all those silky blond curls. When Molly didn't stir, he started to lift her so he could cradle her in his arms.

But Matt didn't get far.

The reinforced walls of the panic room slid open revealing two guards. Both had their silencer-rigged guns aimed right at him.

Hell.

The infrared hadn't picked them up because of the thick steel and concrete. That was Matt's first thought, but it was quickly followed by another one—had Annette set all of this up?

Had she betrayed him?

But Matt didn't have time to come up with possible answers. The guards came out of the panic room and walked closer.

"Put your hands in the air where I can see them," the taller guard ordered. He glanced at the unconscious guard by the sofa. "Step away from the baby."

Because Matt couldn't risk a shootout, he did exactly as ordered. He didn't take just one step from

Molly, he took several so that she wouldn't be in the line of fire. He was in serious trouble here. His only hope was for the guards to get closer so he could incapacitate them.

The shorter guard with buzz-cut black hair went to Matt. The other stayed a "safe" distance on the other side of the room, standing watch to make sure Matt didn't try to pull anything. Matt didn't resist when the guard patted him down and retrieved the Glock from his shoulder holster and the stun gun from his hand.

The taller guard leaned his head to the side and spoke into a grape-size communicator clipped to the collar of his camouflage shirt. "We found your sister's *decorator*," the guy said to the person at the other end of that communicator.

So, there was the answer. Dominic had set this trap because he was suspicious. Matt should have anticipated it.

"What should we do with him?" the guard asked into the communicator.

With the adrenaline surging through him and his pulse crashing in his ears, Matt waited to see what the verdict of this conversation would be.

The smaller guard went through the equipment bag, and of course spotted the infrared monitor and jammer right away. He shot Matt a steely glance. "You might want to take a look at this," he informed his partner. "He's not carrying light."

"Repeat that," the man said into the communicator. A second went by. "Will do."

"Well?" the shorter guard asked. "What do we do with him?"

"Kill him."

Matt didn't react on the outside, but inside his heart kicked up a significant notch. He couldn't die, because that would leave both Molly and Cass to fend for themselves.

The guard tipped his head to the panic room. "We'll kill him in there. No carpet. Less mess to clean up."

With that, the smaller guard used the equipment bag to shove Matt toward the panic room. Matt used the opportunity to do something. He purposely stumbled and dove right toward the guard with the communicator. He needed to take him out first so he couldn't alert Dominic or anyone else.

The stumble ploy worked. Matt plowed into the tall guard and sent both of them crashing to the floor.

But it didn't work for long.

Before Matt could regroup and come up fighting, he felt the end of the gun against the back of his neck. "Move and you die here," the buzz-cut guard warned.

Well, that wasn't much incentive to stay put, especially since the panic room—the place they intended to kill him—was only a few yards away.

The guard he'd tackled got to his feet.

It was as risky a move as he could make, but Matt got ready to slam his elbow into the guy's throat. Of course, the other guard would most likely shoot to kill. But it was the only chance Matt had of getting out of this.

There was a blur of motion, followed by a swoosh of sound. Matt recognized that sound. Not a gun rigged with a silencer.

But a tranquilizer gun.

And that meant Cass was in the room.

The guard with the buzz cut gasped in pain, and he grabbed at the tiny dart that'd gone into his neck.

Matt knew what was going to happen next. The taller guard aimed his gun at the shooter. At Cass.

Before the guy could pull the trigger, Matt dove at the man again and dragged him to the floor. Behind him Matt was aware that Cass was moving. He hoped like hell that she'd stay out of the way.

Matt managed to land a hard punch on the guy's jaw. It was just enough to buy Matt a couple of seconds of time so he could reposition himself and go in for an even harder punch. The third one did the trick, knocking the man unconscious.

To make sure he stayed that way, Matt grabbed the stun gun and gave the guy a jolt, and then he turned his attention to Cass.

"What are you doing here?" he snarled. But, mercy, he was glad to see her.

"Apparently saving your life."

"You picked the handcuff lock." Something he should have anticipated that she'd do. But then, he'd had a lot on his mind, what with the rescue and trying to keep her from being harmed.

"We'll argue about it later," Cass informed him. "Let's take Molly and get out of here."

Matt was all for that.

Until he glanced at the infrared monitor in the equipment bag. There was a group of people moving toward the nursery. At least a half dozen. And with the speed they were coming, Matt had no doubt that these were yet more guards on the way to stop them.

Mercy.

This did not look good.

Matt knew he had only one option.

"Guards are coming. Take Molly," Matt told Cass. "Go through the tunnel in the panic room. Take her to the car and leave. Don't wait for me. I'll catch up with you later."

She shook her head. "What are you planning to do?"

"We need a diversion."

"I'll do that. You take your daughter and get out of here."

That was touching and generous. Cass was offering to make herself bait while Molly and he escaped.

But it wasn't going to happen.

"Take Molly *now*," Matt insisted, pushing her toward the crib. "Before it's too late."

"Come with us."

"I can't. The guards will just follow us into the panic room and trap us in the tunnel."

Oh, she wanted to argue. Matt could see the argument—and plenty of other things—in her eyes. But she must have seen the resolve in his. Or maybe it was the sound of footsteps that made her realize she had to save his daughter.

"Don't you dare get hurt," she warned.

But she did as he ordered. Keeping a firm grip on her tranquilizer gun, she scooped Molly and the baby blanket into her arms and hurried into the panic room.

Matt dove across the room to shut the panic room wall door. In the same motion he grabbed his equipment bag. He got his gun from the unconscious guard and raced to the hall.

He only had to wait a second or two before the first guard rounded the corner.

Matt tucked the equipment bag in his arms, as if he were carrying a baby. And he ran like hell in the opposite direction, leading them away from Cass and Molly.

Matt didn't make it far before the first shot slammed into the wall next to his head.

Chapter Fifteen

Cass heard the panic room wall slide shut behind her. And then she heard the shot.

Sweet heaven, someone had fired a gun.

But she tried not to think about Matt getting trapped, wounded or worse. Right now she had to concentrate on getting to the tunnel so she could escape with Molly. Because if she failed, Matt would be risking his life for nothing.

Since she wasn't sure exactly where that tunnel was, she went to the only other door in the room and tested the knob.

It was locked.

Frantically, she examined the door frame and finally located the tiny button. She pressed it, and the door slid open. It was a tunnel all right. A dark one.

The panic continued while she searched the immediate area for a light switch or a flashlight. Time wasn't on her side, and she had to get out of there before those guards doubled back and realized the baby was missing. At least one or more of those guards would likely know how to get into the panic room.

Cass felt along the wall of the tunnel and practically cheered when she located the switch. She turned it on, fluorescent light spewing down the gray stone walls, and began to run.

Molly stirred in her arms. Cass expected it. The baby's ear was right next to Cass's heart, and she knew for a fact that her heart was pounding like a drum. No one, including a baby, could sleep through that.

She glanced down at the baby to see Molly staring up at her. Molly's bottom lip quivered, and her eyes filled with tears. Oh, no. If she didn't soothe her and fast, Molly was going to cry and alert the guards.

Cass started to hum the first song that came to mind—"Hush Little Baby." It was appropriate for the situation.

It was also useless.

Molly obviously didn't care to heed the song, and her quivering lip turned to a full-fledged cry.

The sound echoed through the tunnel.

Cass shifted the baby to her shoulder and tried to hurry. Not easy to do with a now squirming baby who obviously didn't approve of some stranger taking her out of her crib.

She reached a door at the end of the tunnel, and Cass noticed another tunnel that funneled into this one. It was probably the one that led from the panic room off Dominic's office. She might have to use it if she couldn't get safely outside. Of course, going back inside, especially to Dominic's office, wasn't her first choice to escape, but she might not have a choice.

Cass put her ear to the door to listen for anyone who might be standing guard outside. But it was impossible to hear anything over Molly's cries. So, rather than rush out into the cold and darkness, where anything could be waiting for her, Cass stopped and re-grouped.

First, she tucked her tranquilizer gun in her coat pocket. She didn't want anyone to see the gun and shoot first. In fact, she would go in a surrendering posture just in case.

And then she'd run like crazy to get to the car.

Where hopefully Matt would be waiting. He had to be waiting. He had to be safe and out of the house. Because she couldn't live with the alternative.

When the tranquilizer gun was in place, Cass took a moment to soothe Molly. She didn't have the benefit of experience with caring for nieces or nephews, but she went on instinct. She cradled the little girl close to her, snuggling her inside her coat so she could keep her warm.

"It's all right," Cass whispered. She rocked her gently. "I'm going to keep you safe." And she prayed that she could do just that. "Your daddy is going to be very happy to see you."

Molly's cries softened. So Cass continued, whispering whatever came into her mind. Silly things, like bits of fairy tales and old nursery rhymes.

Finally Molly stopped crying.

She looked up at Cass, blinking hard, and then her eyelids lowered and she fell back asleep.

Cass didn't wait to spring into action. She tested the knob. Another locked door. But because of what she'd gone through in the panic room, she had an easier time finding the mechanism that would unlock it.

She opened the door, slowly, and peered out. The estate was literally lit up like a massive Christmas tree. The wind was howling, swirling snow all around, but there didn't seem to be any guards waiting for them.

She zipped Molly inside her coat so that she'd be protected from the cold, and Cass stepped outside. It took her a moment to get her bearings.

Thankfully the grounds were lit with thousands of tiny colored lights, and she used those lights to navigate her way around the back of the house. She hurried, but it still seemed to take a lifetime to make it to more familiar ground—the garden room. From there it was a straight shot to the car parked in the woods.

In theory, anyway.

She kept near the building, where it was warmer, and she started to cross the recessed porch that served as one of the garden room's entrance.

"Hold it right there," she heard someone say.

Cass froze. She prayed that it was Matt speaking.

But no such luck.

One of Dominic's many guards stepped out from the corner of the garden room. He wore bulky winter clothes, including a parka and ski cap. But what Cass noticed most was the assault rifle. He didn't have it aimed at her. Not yet anyway. However, she didn't doubt he would do just that if she couldn't convince him otherwise.

She decided to go on the offensive, especially since every second that passed was a second that Molly could wake up and start crying again. Best to try to defuse the situation right away.

"I'm in a hurry," she said in a hoarse whisper. Maybe he'd think she had laryngitis and she wouldn't have to explain why she was whispering. "I need to run an errand for Annette."

The guard stepped closer, and she got a better look at him. His long thin face was red from the cold, and his lips were caked with chapped skin. He'd obviously been out there for a while, but it couldn't have been too long in that particular spot, or he would have seen her when she entered the house fifteen minutes earlier. That likely meant he'd been patrolling the grounds, hopefully alone. One guard was more than enough to deal with.

"An errand, you say?" He eyed the lump that Molly was creating in her coat. "Well, why don't I call her to verify that?"

"You could," Cass readily agreed. "She's taking a quick nap before the party and made it clear that she doesn't want to be disturbed. But go ahead and call. I'm sure she won't be that upset when you wake her."

It worked. He stood there and seemed to think about it. But he didn't think long. The man took out his cell phone, and with her luck, Cass figured he was about to call Annette.

"I hope you have another job lined up," Cass mumbled. "Because she's going to fire your butt."

"I'm calling Dominic," he clarified.

Cass's heart went to the ground. This was not what she wanted to happen. And then she felt something that she knew would make this situation go from bad to worse.

Molly squirmed.

If she started to cry or fuss, there was no way that guard would hold her at gunpoint and investigate what she had beneath her coat.

Somehow, she had to get out her tranquilizer gun. Or even, God forbid, her real one that was tucked in the back of her jeans. But either was a huge risk with Molly in her arms. Still, standing there wasn't a safe option, either.

"Mr. Cordova," the guard greeted the person he'd called. Maybe it was Dominic. Or maybe this was some kind of ploy to see how she'd react.

Cass couldn't wait for the man to find out that there was no errand for Annette so she glanced around to figure out what her options were. Her best bet was to run while he was occupied with the call and try to get to the other side of the garden room. Maybe then she could shoot him with the tranquilizer gun when he rounded the corner.

There were a lot of maybes in that scenario, but it beat facing down a gunman while she was holding Matt's baby.

The guard looked at her, and his eyes narrowed. When he reached for his gun, she turned to run. But Cass stopped when she saw the arm reach out from the light-strewn shrubs. That arm vised around the guard's neck, and within seconds the man collapsed onto the ground.

Matt stepped out and hurried to her.

She'd never been happier to see anyone in her life.

"You're alive," she whispered, though her throat had snapped shut, and her voice hardly had any sound. "I heard a shot fired earlier. How did you get out of the house?"

Though he was the answer to her prayers, Matt didn't respond. Instead he caught her and pulled her deeper onto the porch with him. Molly wiggled again. Matt peeked inside the coat to see for himself that his baby was okay.

"Thank you," he whispered to Cass. "Now let's get out of here."

But that thank-you must have tempted fate because they'd only taken a few steps from the cover of the porch when Cass felt something was wrong. She didn't know what exactly. Until she glanced over her shoulder and spotted a man to their right.

Dominic.

He didn't look especially harried, though he'd probably had to run to make his way around the house while dressed in a tux. Still, despite the freezing temperatures and the wind, Dominic managed to look calm and collected.

Except for his gun.

He was carrying a semiautomatic pistol rigged with a silencer. Probably so his guests wouldn't hear their host firing shots.

"Cassandra," he mocked, snaring her gaze. "You're looking lovelier than ever. I love what you've done with your hair."

Matt tried to push her behind him, but it was too late. Dominic lifted his gun and took aim at Matt.

THIS WAS NOT THE WAY Matt wanted his daughter's rescue to play out. Dominic was a dangerous, cold-blooded killer, and he was the last person that Matt wanted involved in this.

Matt kept a firm grip on his Glock and calculated when and how he needed to lunge at the man. His chances of not being shot were slim, but he really didn't have a choice.

"I would like to have an excuse to kill you, Agent Christensen," Dominic warned. Another guard came rushing around the house to join his boss. "But I don't want it to happen here."

Matt froze, not just because of the guard but because of Dominic's comment. "You know who I am?"

He nodded. Smiled. The facial gesture looked totally out of place.

"Mind telling how?" Matt asked.

"It's not important." Dominic turned that frosty gaze back to Cass. "I'm guessing that beneath your coat you have the baby I adopted for my sister. So, without doing anything else that'll make me more irritable than I already am, bundle Molly in your coat and put her on the garden room porch, in the corner."

Matt didn't know what to make of that order. On the one hand, it would take Molly out of the line of fire. But it would also put her out of Matt's reach. When Cass and he finally made a run for it, he would have to figure out how to get Molly.

Next to them, the guard that Matt had choked unconscious stirred, and the man struggled to get to his feet.

"Go inside," Dominic ordered the man. "Later, you can explain to me how you allowed these two to get into the house in the first place."

"We were shorthanded," the guard explained. "You said you wanted everyone searched before they came into the party. That's why there were only two of us back here."

"I said later," Dominic snapped. "Though I doubt your excuse will sound any better then."

Once the guard was back inside, Dominic returned his attention to Cass. "Put the baby on the porch," he repeated, sounding impatient now.

Cass looked at Matt, apparently waiting for him to give her the okay. Matt nodded, and she did as Dominic said. She eased off her coat, careful to keep Molly wrapped snugly inside. His daughter thankfully didn't wake up when Cass placed her on the porch. He hoped the heat seeping from the house would keep her warm, and at least Cass's coat and the porch sheltered from the wind.

"Thank you for being concerned about Molly's safety," Cass remarked. But there was no gratitude in her voice. Just hatred for the man who'd destroyed her life.

Dominic shook his head. "Me, concerned for Molly? Not on your pathetic little life. The only reason I adopted the kid was because Annette kept harping about it. So, being the good brother that I am, I conceded. And look where it got me."

Though it was freezing, Matt could practically feel his blood boil over at that. This was his child, more precious to him than life itself, and Dominic didn't care one iota about her.

"The adoption was illegal," Cass pointed out.

Why, Matt didn't know, but he didn't think he would like where this conversation was going.

Dominic nodded and brushed away some snow-flakes that whirled onto his face. "A pity, that. Because without the adoption, Special Agent Christensen wouldn't be on my estate causing me such distress." His oily smile returned. "But then, perhaps neither would you, Cassandra. And unlike the agent here, I very much wanted to see you."

"The feeling's not mutual," Cass fired back.

Matt nudged her arm with his equipment bag,

hoping it would keep her quiet. He didn't want her to egg Dominic on, especially since he needed her focused on what had to be done. Somehow he had to tackle that guard and Dominic at the same time.

But Cass didn't stay quiet.

"What did you do with the surveillance disks that prove you're a killer?" she asked.

"You tell me. They're missing."

"Yes, and you put them someplace I wouldn't find them."

He clucked his tongue. "I have better things to do with my time than cover tracks that don't need to be covered. Perhaps you haven't heard—the authorities like me these days."

"Oh, I've heard," Cass grumbled. "But that has nothing to do with Molly. You've already said you don't care about the baby. And I doubt you care that Agent Christensen came here to collect his child. I'm the one you want."

Dominic's eyebrow lifted. "True. So, what do you have in mind?"

"Let him take Molly. Let them leave. Then, you can call the local sheriff and have him arrest me."

His eyebrow lifted higher, and amusement danced over his face. "You're trading your life for theirs?"

"No. She's not," Matt snarled. And he gave Cass another nudge.

"Think of Molly," she said to him. "She's already lost her mother. She needs you. I'm the expendable one here."

"Not just expendable," Dominic agreed. "You're the grand prize, Cass. I accept your generous but incredibly stupid offer. Always thinking with your heart. When you will ever learn?"

She hiked up her chin. "At least I have a heart."

Tired of this posturing and dangerous verbal game, Matt took a step forward. "I'm withdrawing her offer. Let Cass leave with Molly."

"Oh, this is so touching." Dominic shook his head. "I'm afraid I can't accept that arrangement. I'll allow one thing and one thing only—Agent Christensen, pick up your baby and walk away from this. Cassandra and I have some very important business to finish."

Dominic pointed his gun at Cass.

"My advice," Dominic added, glancing at Matt, "get out of here *now.* Save your little blond-haired baby while you can."

God, it was tempting, but he couldn't do it. He couldn't let Cass face this monster alone. "I'm not leaving without Cass."

"Yes, you are," Cass insisted.

"You should listen to her," Dominic verified. "Because she knows what I'm capable of doing. It's cold, and I have no desire to stay out here any longer. Thirty seconds—that's all you have, Agent Christensen, to put your heroism aside and get the hell out of here with your baby."

"And if I don't?" Matt challenged.

Dominic shrugged. "Simple. I kill Cass and you both."

Chapter Sixteen

"Thirty seconds," Cass repeated to herself.

Not much time for Matt to make the most critical decision of his life. She'd have to help him along with this, or Dominic would do exactly what he promised to do. Kill them both. And if he needed any help doing that, he had one of his armed minions by his side.

"I *really* want you to go," she said to Matt. Her teeth were chattering, but the cold hadn't dulled her senses. She was well aware how this was going to have to play out.

"No," was Matt's answer.

Cass wanted to force him to get out of there. She wanted to smash her fist into Dominic's face. But more than anything, she wanted Matt and Molly to be safe.

"Twenty seconds," Dominic announced, checking his watch. "Time's just flying by."

Cass cursed at him and looked up at Matt, pleading with him to do what was best for Molly.

But he ignored her nonverbal cues, leaned in and whispered, "Drop to the ground now."

She pulled back, so her eyes could meet his.

"Now," he repeated.

He didn't say it with anger, nor was it heavy with emotion. Though she knew the emotion and fear were there. He said it like a trained agent who knew what he was doing.

"Trust me," he whispered.

"Ten seconds," Dominic called out.

Cass took a second or two to decide what to do, but she really didn't have a choice. She couldn't draw her weapon, not with the baby in her arms. She needed both hands just to hold on to Molly. So, she could either try to talk Dominic out of his thirty-second death sentence. Or she could go along with Matt. And that meant she could only do one thing.

She dropped to the ground.

Her hands were practically numb from the cold, but when she dropped and rolled toward the shrubs, Cass yelled for Matt to get down, and she drew her gun.

Matt did get down. Thank heaven. He dropped to the snow-littered ground, as well. In the opposite direction from where she was.

The fall was hard. And Dominic made it harder.

Dominic got off a shot before Matt did.

Cass glanced at Matt for a split second to make sure he hadn't been hit. He hadn't, but Dominic's bullet had knocked the Glock from Matt's hand. Matt was a sitting duck. He scrambled to the side, taking cover behind a marble birdbath, just before Dominic fired another shot.

She concentrated on the guard, who was concentrating on her. Specifically, he was positioning his rifle so he could shoot her.

But Cass shot first.

Her gun might have been a lot smaller than his, but it did the trick. The bullet smashed into the guard's right wrist. He howled in pain and dropped the rifle to the ground.

Cass didn't have time to celebrate her victory.

Because Dominic pulled the trigger again.

The silenced shot swooshed through the air, and it slammed into the icy ground kicking up frozen dirt and snow. But at least it didn't hit Matt. No thanks to Dominic. His aim had been dead on, but Matt had jumped out of the way at the last possible second.

Since Matt couldn't get to his Glock, Cass was about to take aim at Dominic, but the guard she'd shot went after his rifle again. She fired at him, not intending to kill him. She didn't want to have to live with that, but she didn't want Matt or her to die, either. She shot at the man's other arm, and her stomach turned when the bullet made the intended contact.

The man crawled away from his rifle and took cover at the side of the building. Cass watched to make sure he didn't go after Molly. If he did, this time she would shoot to kill, and she wouldn't regret it.

"Stop!" someone yelled.

But Matt didn't stop. From the cover of the birdbath, he'd already taken aim at Dominic. Matt's bullet slammed into Dominic's right shoulder. He hardly reacted, aiming at Matt again.

"I said stop it!" the person shouted. That shout was followed by a shot fired from a silencer.

Cass soon saw the source.

Annette was in her motorized wheelchair, and she was at the corner of the house with gun in hand, aimed into the air.

Dressed in a silky black party dress speckled with crystals and no coat, Annette looked frozen, but that didn't stop her from maneuvering herself between Dominic and Matt. Dominic didn't fire at Matt, but he didn't lower his gun, either.

"Where's Molly?" Annette demanded.

Cass tipped her head to the porch, and Annette immediately looked in that direction, where Molly was still thankfully sleeping.

"This ends now," Annette said first to her brother. Then, she looked at Cass. "Both of you drop your guns."

Dominic didn't take his eyes off Matt. Nor did he clamp his hand over his shoulder to slow down the bleeding. He just stood there. "It's not over, Annette. This has nothing to do with you. Get inside now."

"No. I've turned a blind eye to things you've done in the past, but now you've endangered my baby, and I won't stand still for that."

"She's not your baby," Dominic tossed at her. And Cass could tell from the gleefulness in his eyes that he was up to something. "Molly is Agent Christensen's daughter. The adoption was illegal, and he's here to take her away from you."

There was no glee in Annette's eyes. "This is Agent Matt Christensen?" she asked, her voice trembling now. She moved her wheelchair back so that she was by her brother's side instead of in front of him.

"In the flesh," Dominic confirmed.

It was a definite glare that Annette sent Matt's way. Now she lowered her gun as if preparing to use it on Matt.

So, this was Dominic's plan—to get his sister to kill Matt.

But two could play at this dangerous game.

"Molly shouldn't have to live here under the same roof with your brother," Cass said to Annette. "You know that. That's why you were planning on leaving. So you could get Molly away from him."

Now it was Dominic's turn to glare. At his sister. "You were going to leave?" he asked through clenched teeth.

"You were bringing that dangerous man to the house," Annette said. But her glare cooled significantly. Whether it was love for her brother or fear of him, it was obvious that Annette was still lacking some backbone.

"Go ahead," Dominic said to his sister. "Kill Agent Christensen. I'll take care of his *partner.* Then there'll be no one to challenge you for custody of Molly."

"If you kill me, you'll be just like your brother," Matt insisted.

Annette frantically shook her head. "No. I'm not like him. But I can't let you have Molly, either. You gave her up—"

"I didn't. After her mother died, someone stole Molly so that Dominic could adopt her. I didn't know she existed."

Matt inched toward his gun. It was a huge risk. Especially since Dominic was volleying his attention among Annette, Matt and her. And unlike Matt, Dominic still had a gun.

But then, so did Cass.

"Move and I'll kill Cassandra," Dominic warned Matt. He turned the gun on her.

Annette issued her own silent warning to Matt. She aimed her pistol at him. Cass wasn't sure the woman had the nerve to fire, but her hand was shaking so violently that she just might accidentally pull that trigger and hurt Matt.

Cass tried to keep watch on both of them. She didn't want to shoot Annette, but she would.

The four of them stood there, for long agonizing seconds. There were no party sounds at this end of the estate. No human sounds at all. Only the wind.

Until Molly woke up.

Cass saw the squirmy movement in her coat, braced herself, waiting for the ensuing cry.

That cry changed everything.

Annette snapped her head in the direction of the baby. Dominic made his own move. She could see he was about to pull the trigger and shoot Matt, who scrambled toward his own gun.

All hell broke loose.

Dominic started firing.

THIS WAS MATT'S NIGHTMARE come true.

Molly and Cass were in danger, and he couldn't get to his gun to save them.

Thankfully Cass dove back into the shrubs so she'd have some small amount of cover. It wasn't enough. Not nearly enough, considering that Dominic was firing at them. It also didn't help that Molly was crying and that Annette was screaming for everyone to stop while she tried to crawl onto the porch to get to the baby.

But Dominic didn't stop.

Matt crouched down behind the birdbath, forcing himself to stay put, because he wouldn't be much good to Cass and Molly if he was dead. And he counted shots. When all ten rounds had been fired, Dominic tossed it aside and shoved his hand inside his tux jacket for his back-up weapon, no doubt.

That was Matt's cue to come out of cover and grab his own gun several yards away. But Dominic was fast. He had his pistol drawn and ready.

Matt heard the shot, just as his hand closed over his weapon. And he figured it was too late to stop Dominic.

Matt braced himself for the feel of the bullet that would no doubt slam into his body.

It didn't.

His gaze whipped to Cass. God, had she been shot? But she appeared to be unharmed, except for a look of pure terror on her face.

Matt had expected that Dominic would keep firing his backup weapon until he was sure that Cass and he were dead. But he accepted the miracle that he was still alive, lifted his Glock and aimed at Dominic.

Only Dominic wasn't firing.

His hand and his gun were at his side, and there was a puzzled look on his face. He turned, glancing over his shoulder. That glance was his last voluntary move.

Dominic collapsed onto the ground.

Matt soon realized why. Annette was behind him, on the ground where she'd obviously fallen from her wheelchair. But the fall hadn't released her grip on her own gun. And it was literally smoking.

She'd shot her brother.

"He could have hurt Molly," Annette said. "He could have hurt Molly."

"Watch out for that guard," Cass warned when Matt stood. But the guard that she'd wounded earlier stepped out from the side of the estate, and he had his hands lifted in the air in surrender.

"Go to Molly," Cass insisted. "I'll take care of him."

Matt did go toward his still-crying daughter, but he stopped first to retrieve Dominic's gun. Matt kicked it out of the man's reach. Just in case. But it wasn't necessary. When he pressed his fingers to Dominic's neck, he couldn't get even a thread of pulse.

"He's dead?" Annette asked. She was as pale as the snow and was shivering.

Matt nodded, sending Annette over the edge. She dropped the gun and began to sob. He'd take care of her later, but right now he had to get to his daughter, to make sure she hadn't been harmed.

As if she were fragile and might shatter in his hands, he lifted her and eased back the edge of Cass's coat so he could see Molly's face. Yes, she was crying, but it obviously wasn't tears of pain. He kissed her tear-soaked cheek and pulled her to him. To keep her warm. And because he needed to hold her as much as she apparently needed to be held.

Matt could have sworn his heart doubled in size.

"Dominic could have hurt her," Annette repeated through her sobs. She crawled to her brother and cradled him in her arms, like Matt was doing to Molly.

Cass made her way to the guard, and Matt heard her order the guy to take off his pants so she could use them to tie him up. It was a good temporary measure, but the guy's hand was bleeding. He'd need medical attention. For that matter so did Annette. She was in shock and would need to be checked for exposure to the elements. He wanted Molly checked as well.

He also needed to call the local sheriff.

Matt wasn't sure how all of this would play out, but there'd be an investigation. Once he had Molly away from the estate, he could concentrate on keeping Cass out of jail.

Molly's cries turned to whimpers, but she didn't go back to sleep. She stared up, studying him. Matt couldn't help it. He studied her, too, and knew that he'd never grow tired of looking at her face.

"Is she okay?" Cass asked. She kept a vigilant watch of their surroundings as she made her way to him.

Matt nodded and because the wind actually seemed to be getting colder, he stepped inside the garden room. Once Cass was inside, he handed Molly to her.

"I'll get Annette," he told Cass. "And then I need to call the sheriff."

Their eyes met. A thousand things passed between them, including regret that despite all the hell they'd been through, she still didn't have what she needed to clear her name. And with Dominic dead, it might be even harder to prove that she wasn't a killer.

"Is the sheriff someone we can trust?" she asked.

"Yes." He couldn't say the same for the federal agents who might be sent in as well, but he would be there to run interference if needed.

"It'll be okay," Cass whispered. She tipped her head toward Annette and nuzzled Molly's cheek. His daughter seemed to like the attention she was getting.

Matt kissed them both. It was a moment, all right. One he'd remember forever. Cass, standing there holding his daughter. His daughter, looking at him as if he might actually have some answers.

But the moment couldn't last.

He had a chore to do. And he wasn't looking forward to it.

Matt walked outside, and though Annette put up a feeble fight about leaving her brother, Matt carried her inside anyway. Once he deposited her in a chaise lounge, he went back out for the guard. He dragged the man into the garden room and kept his Glock ready just in case Dominic had any other hired guns lurking about.

Because he knew he couldn't put it off any longer, Matt took out his phone to call 911.

"It's okay," Cass assured him.

But he wasn't so sure of that. Matt actually considered not making that call. Cass, Molly and he could walk out of here, go to the car and drive away.

"You don't want to be on the run with Molly," Cass said, apparently reading his mind. "Call the sheriff."

"I wish I could think of another way to do this."

"Me, too." Cass rose up on her toes and kissed him.

She broke the kiss and tipped her head to the phone. "Do it before you change your mind."

Matt did. He called Sheriff Mike Medina, in the little town of Rim Rock, and gave the man a brief recap of what'd happened. Then he requested an ambulance for the injured guard. He also suggested that Medina bring any and all backup with him, just in case.

"He's on the way," Matt relayed to Cass. "He says because of the snow, it'll take him about twenty minutes to get here."

"Not much time," she mumbled under her breath.

Matt looked into the coat-blanket and saw that Molly had fallen back asleep. Obviously, this ordeal hadn't bothered her. Thank God. However, he couldn't say the same for Cass.

And that gave him an idea.

"We have twenty minutes," Matt reiterated. "We could wait here for the sheriff, or we could look in Dominic's office and see if those disks are there."

Her eyes widened. "You think they might be?"

"We'll never know unless we look."

She glanced at the guard and Annette. "What about them? You think it's okay to leave them alone?"

"Under normal circumstances, I'd say no. But we're no safer here than we would be in Dominic's office."

And there was another reason to go to the office: Matt was concerned that some evidence might be suppressed or even destroyed if someone in the department tried to cover up the deals that'd been made with Dominic.

"What about other guards?" Cass asked. "What if they see us?"

Matt shrugged. "We'll tell them that Annette killed Dominic, and that the sheriff is on the way. That should cause them to hightail it out of here, since I figure most if not all have criminal records. Also, if something goes wrong, we can always use Dominic's panic room and wait there until the sheriff arrives."

Cass still gave it some thought. So did Matt. It wasn't risk proof, but it probably wasn't any riskier than waiting around in a glass-walled garden room with Annette and a guard.

"Okay," she said. "I'll search while you keep an eye out so that no one sneaks up on us. I've had enough confrontations and shootouts to last me a lifetime."

So had he.

Matt took the infrared monitor from the equipment bag and led the way to Dominic's office. As they neared the center of the house, he could hear sounds from the party. Music, laughter, conversation. Apparently, no one knew yet that their host was lying dead in the yard. But they soon would. Matt only hoped there was enough time to find those disks.

He opened the office door. The room was dark, and he kept it that way until Cass and he stepped inside. Then he shut and locked the door behind them before he turned on the light.

"Don't move."

Matt turned to his right, and found himself looking down the barrel of a gun.

Chapter Seventeen

Cass forced herself not to reach for her gun. Not that she could have. The way she was holding Molly, both hands were occupied. And that wasn't good.

Because Libby was holding them at gunpoint.

"Matt," Libby said on a rise of breath. She quickly lowered her gun. "God, you two gave me a scare."

"I could say the same. What are you doing in here?"

"Looking for evidence to convict Dominic. I don't agree with the departmental policy of offering deals to men like him. I decided to befriend Dominic so I could wrangle an invitation to this party and search his office."

Cass glanced around the room and spotted the large, black, woman's leather purse on Dominic's desk. It wasn't an accessory that went with Libby's dark-amber silk party dress, and Cass could see some surveillance disks stuffed inside it.

"Dominic's dead," Matt informed Libby.

Her eyes widened. "You killed him?"

"No. His sister did."

Libby nodded, swallowed hard, and nodded again. "Well, I guess my trip was wasted." She went to the desk and began to zip the leather bag.

Matt reached out and snagged her wrist. "What are those?"

Libby made a sound of dismissal and eased out of his grip. "Surveillance disks that Gideon asked me to get. I'm taking them to him."

Cass shifted Molly in her arms so she could have a better look. "The disks are dated the same day and time that Dominic murdered his partner."

"Yes," Libby readily admitted.

"Except for these," Matt pointed out, running his finger over the bottom two disks. "These are from a week ago."

"Gideon didn't tell me why he wanted them." Libby looked at her. "Maybe so he can destroy any evidence that would exonerate you."

Libby held Cass's stare a moment before she resumed zipping her purse.

"How do you know me?" Cass asked. "We've never met."

Another sound of dismissal. "You look exactly like the photo circulating through various agencies in the Justice Department. Now, if you'll excuse me, I have to go. Gideon wouldn't want me to be caught up in a murder investigation. You've called the sheriff, I suppose?"

"Of course. He'll be here soon," Matt explained. "And I think it's a good idea if he sees those disks first. Including the ones from a week ago. In fact, maybe I could have a look at those now."

Libby held on tightly to the purse. "Gideon wouldn't approve. Nor would I. You're on suspension, Matt. Best if you stay out of this so you don't taint any evidence."

"My goal isn't to taint anything. I just want the truth." He took out the infrared monitor and held it up for her to see. "Notice something odd?" He didn't wait for her to answer. "You didn't show up on the monitor."

Cass did not have a good feeling about this, and she began to back away so that she could put some distance between Molly and Libby.

"The monitor probably malfunctioned," Libby answered.

"That's one explanation. But not a good one. A better explanation is that you're wearing a thermal armor device to block the infrared."

"Why would I do that?" And she seemed surprised that he would even suggest such a thing.

Cass backed farther away, toward the wall. And her position also gave her a different angle to view the desk. Specifically, the chair.

And the small device sitting on it.

"Matt," Cass managed to say through her suddenly clamped throat. "I think there's a bomb in the chair."

Matt looked, and judging from the stark expression

that came over him, it was indeed a bomb. But that brief look was costly.

Libby pulled out something from her pocket. Not a gun. But some kind of small metal tube. She slammed it into Matt's stomach and then pulled out her gun. She aimed it at them.

Matt staggered and caught onto the desk.

Cass couldn't believe what she was seeing. Her heart began to race out of control.

"What did you do to him?" Cass hurried to him and stopped him falling. Barely. But he was weak, as if he no longer had control of his muscles.

"I used a new kind of tranquilizer, but it doesn't work as well through winter clothes so he'll only be dazed for a couple of minutes," Libby said, moving toward the door. "I really hate to do this, but I don't have a choice. Self-preservation is a strong motivator."

"You're not going to survive if that bomb goes off," Cass pointed out.

"Oh, it won't detonate for another four minutes, and I intend to be gone by then. Timing is everything."

Four minutes.

That wasn't nearly enough.

Cass looked around for the nearest exit. There was the door. Or a trio of windows. Libby was blocking the door, and those windows were on the other side of the room. Libby would likely shoot her before she could reach them.

"What about Matt, Molly and me?" Cass asked.

"What about the other guests? You're willing to let us all die?"

"The guests will be fine. Probably. The bomb is only meant to destroy what's in this room. I didn't have time to sanitize the place, and I couldn't risk the department or the locals finding something."

"Something that would incriminate you," Matt mumbled. He moved, grunting at the exertion and managed to sit up, though he was still unsteady.

"What can I say? I'm human. Dominic offered me a lot of money. A bribe to give him information about the department's investigation. He badgered me until I accepted it. And then he tried to blackmail me."

"I could have told you he was a snake," Cass managed to say. And she hoped she could distract Libby enough so she could overpower her and take that gun.

But how?

She couldn't do much with Molly in her arms.

"I don't doubt that snake part, now," Libby concurred. "The reason I have to blow up this room is because Dominic made sure that my DNA is somewhere on the floor, and I don't have time to clean it up. There's no reasonable explanation I can give to Gideon as to why I'd have sex with Dominic, someone I wasn't supposed to have even met until yesterday."

"You had sex with him?" Cass asked. "Here? Bad idea. He records everything."

"Spare the lecture. I underestimated him, and I have

to clean up my mess. That includes destroying the disks that could prove I was here. Now, here's the deal I'm offering you," Libby continued. "You have three minutes left, and I need a minute of that to get to a safe part of the estate. Give me the baby, and I'll get her to safety. But you and Matt, well, I can't allow you to live because you're witnesses. Make your decision quick. There isn't much time, and I wouldn't want Molly to get hurt or worse with flying debris in the explosion."

The threat, and it was a threat, caused the anger to spear through Cass. There was no way she'd trust this lying scheming witch with an innocent little baby. Turning to the side so that Molly would be shielded from Libby, Cass rammed her forearm across the objects on the desk. Pens, paperweights and files went flying.

Libby whirled around, aiming her gun, but Cass dropped to the wooden floor. Cradling Molly from the impact, she landed hard on her butt. So hard that it nearly knocked the breath from her. But it didn't matter. The distraction had worked.

Matt managed to latch on to Libby's leg, and with a fierce growl, he dragged her to the floor.

The two of them fell against the desk, shoving it across the floor and ramming it into the chair. Cass watched in horror as the chair tipped over.

And the bomb dropped.

Cass called out for Matt to get down, but he was in a fight for his life, and he barely had any strength. He probably didn't even hear her. She instinctively rolled over so the baby would be protected. Molly woke up and began to cry.

There was a crash. More of a thud. And she realized Libby and Matt had crashed into the door.

The device hadn't gone off.

The relief she felt only lasted a split-second because Cass saw the timer. Less than two minutes. Oh, God. Was that even enough time to get Molly to safety, especially with Libby and Matt blocking the door?

Cass couldn't risk it.

Obviously Matt knew that, as well, because he said with slurred speech, "Save Molly."

Cass intended to do just that, even though the thought of leaving Matt behind broke her heart. Still, she couldn't risk Molly's life.

She remembered that Annette had said Dominic had a panic room. She hurried to the corner, located the tiny button. When she pressed it, the reinforced steel door slid open just as it'd done in the nursery.

Cass worked as fast as she could. She put the baby inside the panic room, and prayed the steel walls would protect her from the explosion. But she couldn't rely on the walls alone. Plus, she had no intention of leaving Matt out there with that bomb.

She raced to the window, found the latch and shoved it open. Just touching the bomb turned her stomach, but she picked it up and tossed it out the window.

Still, it wouldn't be enough.

The seconds were ticking off in her head.

They had less than a minute.

She went to help Matt, just as he slammed his fist into Libby's jaw. He was obviously still weak from the tranquilizer, but that punch sent Libby crashing into the wall.

Cass didn't bother to see if the woman was okay. She latched onto Matt's arm and pulled him toward the panic room. "The bomb's about to go off."

That seemed to give him the jolt of energy he needed. Matt maneuvered her ahead of him, shoving her into the panic room. He reached for the button to close the door.

But Libby got to her feet.

And aimed her gun at them.

Matt stabbed the button and dragged Cass to the floor. But Libby fired. Before the doors could close. And the bullet crashed into the wall behind them. Thankfully, it was her only shot because the doors slammed shut.

Only then did Cass realize she'd left the disks behind. It was too late and far too risky to go back after them. Besides, every second counted.

"Go to the tunnel," Matt ordered.

Because his arms were still affected by the tranquilizer, Cass scooped up Molly, and they ran as if their lives depended on it. Because it did.

Matt didn't stop. He didn't slow down. He hooked his arm around her waist, and they raced into the mouth of the steel-gray tunnel.

Behind him, the blast tore through the walls and the door.

MATT SHOVED OPEN the tunnel door and pushed Molly and Cass into the open. Away from any debris that might shoot down through the tunnel.

He succeeded.

They got outside, into the freezing air. But the detonation hadn't been quiet. Obviously, the guests had heard the noise, and there were frantic shouts and the sounds of vehicles speeding away from the estate.

"We made it," Cass said through rough breaths. She threw Molly and herself into Matt's arms.

Yes. But it might take a decade or so before Matt's heartbeat could return to normal. He'd come close to losing them.

"Libby." He cursed under his breath. "I can't believe what she did."

"You think she's alive?" Cass asked.

"I doubt it." Still, it was a chance he couldn't take. After all, everything else had gone wrong tonight.

And then he heard a sound he actually wanted to hear. A police siren.

"Come on," Matt said. "Let's go back to the garden room and wait there for the sheriff."

Since Cass was coatless and shivering, she quickly agreed. While Matt kept his gun ready, they made their way through the winter assault to the garden room.

The siren grew closer, but Matt saw something through the glass walls that was not welcome.

Ronald and Gideon were there, waiting.

Neither the guard nor Annette had moved. In fact,

Annette was rocking, staring straight ahead as if seeing nothing. Someone, Ronald probably, had tended to the guard's wounds. And both Ronald and Gideon were definitely standing guard.

Ronald opened the door for them. "Are you all okay?"

Matt didn't answer. After what they'd been through tonight, all he could do was keep a close watch on Ronald and Gideon.

"Libby might be dead," Matt informed them. He stepped inside, keeping himself in front of Cass and Molly. Molly, too, had apparently had enough of this because she started to fuss.

Gideon stepped toward him, but his attention soon landed on Cass. Judging from the way he bunched up his forehead, he wasn't happy to see her.

"Libby *is* dead," Gideon explained. "Her body is in the hall just outside what's left of Dominic's office. What happened?"

"She took a bribe from Dominic, and then he tried to blackmail her. She stole the surveillance disks that would have proved her guilt—and Cass's innocence."

"You personally saw what was on the disks?" Gideon asked.

Matt really hated to admit this. "No. But Libby admitted that she'd accepted money from Dominic, and then she tried to kill us."

Gideon shoved his hands into the pockets of his tux

pants. "So, Libby was the one who sent those assassins after you."

"How would she have known to do that?" Matt wanted to know.

"Through the leak she'd established in communications. When you started asking questions about Molly and the adoption, Libby was probably concerned that you'd come to Dominic's estate to get your child, and in doing so, you'd find out that she was on Dominic's payroll." Gideon shook his head. "I knew the person responsible for the leak and the havoc was someone close to me, but until tonight I didn't know who."

"Well, now you know," Matt practically snarled. "Too bad you didn't find out sooner. It would have saved Cass and me a lot of grief."

"Yes." Gideon paused. "I'm sorry about that. And I'm sorry about what I have to do next."

Gideon walked closer, so that he could face Cass. "Cassandra Harrison, you're under arrest."

Chapter Eighteen

"Christmas morning," Cass mumbled as she watched the sun rise.

A white Christmas, at that. No more howling wind. No more gray skies. It was sunny, and the snow had frosted the landscape. Everything was fresh, festive and glittering.

Well, except her own situation.

Talk about pure irony.

Dominic was dead, no longer a threat to her, and yet here she sat in the Rim Rock county jail. And she wasn't alone. Sheriff Medina was nearby in his office, which was just across the hall from her locked cell. The sheriff was on the phone and had been most of the night. He was getting updates from the Texas Rangers and Justice Department agents who'd been called in to process the crime scene.

Ronald, too, was in the sheriff's office, also on the phone getting updates from Gideon. Judging from the parts of the conversation that Cass could hear, Gideon was still at the crime scene.

Molly was in a carrier seat on the sheriff's desk, next to a small fake Christmas tree. She was asleep. *Finally.* Matt had spent a good portion of the night trying to soothe and feed her, all the while making calls that would set Cass free.

He hadn't succeeded.

Around 5:00 a.m., everyone had realized that Molly wouldn't have enough formula and diapers to make it through the day. Since the town's only grocery store was closed for Christmas, Matt had decided to drive back to the estate to get some.

Cass checked the massive wall clock to the right of the sheriff's door. It was just after 7:30, which meant Matt had been gone for way too long—especially considering that it only took twenty minutes to get to the estate.

She turned away from the tiny barred window and cleared her throat to get Ronald's attention. "Could you please check on Matt?"

"I just tried to call him, but there was no answer. There are a lot of dead spots out here where there's no reception."

Cass hadn't thought she could feel any lower, but that did it. "He could have been in an accident. The roads haven't been plowed yet."

Ronald stood and walked across the hall to her cell. Probably so he wouldn't have to speak loudly and risk waking Molly. "Matt knows how to drive in snow."

Yes. But that didn't relieve her concerns for his safety and for the investigation.

For everything.

Maybe it was the fact that it was Christmas morning and she was in a jail cell, but Cass couldn't help but think about her future.

If she even had one.

The disks had likely been destroyed in the explosion. So there was no proof to exonerate her. But no Dominic to point a finger at her, either. Still, maybe the Justice Department would use Dominic's deposition or something.

In other words, she might stay in jail for the rest of her life.

"Annette's being taken to a psychiatric hospital," Ronald informed her. "She appears to have had a total breakdown."

Cass had expected that. After all, the woman had killed her own brother.

"There isn't any evidence to arrest Dominic's new business partner," Ronald continued. "But we'll put some agents on him. Eventually, he'll make a wrong step."

Cass didn't care one iota about that. He was the reason the Justice Department had made the deal with Dominic. And that was the reason they weren't working hard to clear her name.

"Shouldn't you go out and look for Matt?" she asked.

Ronald's mouth flattened. "He knows how to drive in snow."

"So you've said."

"And I'm not supposed to leave you," Ronald added. "Gideon's orders. He thinks you might try to escape."

She tipped her head toward Molly. "Not on your life. Do you really think I'd risk you or the sheriff trying to shoot at me with Matt's baby just one room away?"

His flattened mouth softened a bit. "You really care for that little girl."

"Yes." And Cass hadn't known just how much until she said it aloud. "Matt won't have any trouble keeping custody of her, will he?"

"No. The adoption was illegal. He said he'll file for temporary custody tomorrow. Then, once he has proven paternity, custody will be permanent."

Good. That was something at least—Matt would be able to raise his daughter without a legal battle.

"What about the gunman I shot?" Cass asked. "Will he be okay?"

Ronald lifted his eyebrow. "He'll be fine. I'm just surprised that you're concerned about him."

"Despite what you think of me, I don't enjoy shooting people." Other images of a shooting went through her mind. "Did Matt tell you about the other guard, the one in the bushes?"

"He did. Clearly a case of self-defense."

That was good, too. Another good thing that she could add—no one seemed ready and willing to arrest Matt for anything that'd happened. As difficult as it was for Cass to be behind bars, it made her life much easier to know that Matt would be free. And happy with his daughter.

Molly made a small sound of protest, and Cass immediately stepped to the side so she could see the carrier. The baby had obviously woken up. She didn't wake up quietly, either. She began to cry.

Ronald hurried back across the hall to pick her up. He also took her out of the office, probably so her cries wouldn't interrupt the sheriff's phone conversation.

"It's okay, sweetheart," Cass assured her when Ronald came closer. Cass felt the outside of Molly's diaper. "She's wet."

Ronald looked as if she'd just announced the end of the world.

"Get me a diaper and open this cell door," Cass suggested.

Ronald stood there, volleying glances between a crying Molly and her. Molly's cries won out because he grabbed the key from the sheriff's desk, a diaper, and he opened the cell door.

Cass didn't know which gave her more relief—hearing that door open or having Molly placed in her arms. Just holding Molly made her smile.

She wasn't exactly a pro at changing a baby, but Cass quickly figured it out. Molly squirmed and fought the process a little, but in the end Cass managed. Well, for the most part. The little swatches of tape that held the diaper in place were askew.

When she was done, Cass pulled the baby to her

chest and rocked her. Molly settled down almost immediately. The moment was perfect. Almost.

Then she heard the front door open. No winter rush
of wind, but there were footsteps. She held her breath.
And was rewarded when Matt came down the corridor.
He had a diaper bag in one hand and his equipment bag
in the other.

He smiled when he saw her holding Molly, and Cass
smiled, too. Things weren't perfect yet, but they were
getting there.

"I was worried about you," she confessed.

"Sorry. Things just took a little longer than I'd
planned." He stepped into the cell and sat on the cot
next to them. "Before the battery on my phone died, I
arranged for a flight to San Antonio."

"Oh." There went her near-perfect feeling. "Well,
that's great. A jail isn't any place for a baby." Her heart
was breaking, but she forced herself to keep things
light. "Besides, I'm not very good at diapering."

Matt took his daughter and inspected Cass's work.
"Neither of us is good at it."

Molly didn't make a sound. She sat there in her
daddy's lap and stared at him. Ronald must have
decided he had something to do because he went back
into the sheriff's office. So, with the exception of the
phone conversation and Cass's own heart pounding in
her ears, the place was silent.

Uncomfortably silent.

"You're going to make a great father," she said.

"I talked to Gideon," he said at the same moment.

Cass's heart slowed significantly. "And?"

"The jail was for your own safety. Gideon was afraid that one of Dominic's guards might still be loyal to him even after death."

It took awhile for Cass to grasp that. "So, am I under arrest?"

He shook his head. "There'll be an investigation, but when the dust settles, I don't think anyone will take what Dominic had said over your word."

The air just sort of swooshed out of her lungs, and Cass went limp with relief. She dropped her head on Matt's shoulder and got a pat on the cheek from Molly. She got an even nicer gift from Matt.

He kissed her.

It was sweet and warm. And short. Molly reached out and batted them with her tiny hand.

"So, what do you think?" Matt asked his daughter. "Would you like Cass for a mom?"

Molly grinned and pumped her legs and arms.

"That's a yes," Matt concluded. He turned to Cass. "And what about you—would you like to be Molly's mom?"

Cass didn't even have to think about it. "More than anything."

"Anything?" he questioned. "Because I was hoping that you'd want me to go along with this Mommy and Molly package."

Oh, mercy. A slow heartbeat. Now, a fast one. And

it took her several moments just to speak. "More than anything," she repeated. "I'm in love with you."

"Really?" he asked, as if that were a surprise.

She nodded. "Back at the estate, when I thought I'd lost you, I knew I couldn't lose you."

All right. That wasn't exactly the way Cass meant to say it. She wasn't making sense, but she could feel. Every inch of her knew this was right. Matt made it even more right by kissing her again. This one wasn't sweet and warm. It was long and hot.

The kind of kiss to seal promises made for life.

Matt pulled away from her and ran his tongue over his bottom lip. "Hmm." And he smiled. It was a naughty smile. One that made her think of what she wanted to do to him once they were alone. "You taste…"

"Expensive?" she provided.

"No."

Cass smiled. "Happy?"

Matt shook his head. "You taste like the woman I love."

The words made it all the way to her heart.

Cass gathered her family into her arms and kissed them both.

* * * * *

Look for Delores Fossen's Newborn Conspiracy, *the next book in the* FOR THEIR BABY'S SAKE *series, coming in December 2008 from Mills & Boon® Intrigue.*

Mills & Boon® Intrigue
brings you a sneak preview of…

Caridad Piñeiro's Devotion Calls

Ricardo Fernandez has the power to heal
people. But he also has one golden rule – never
get entangled in the private lives of people who
come to him for help. Despite this, Ricardo can't
avoid his attraction to Sara Martinez, a nurse
who has brought her terminally ill mother to
him for treatment. As the pair embark on a dark
adventure, could Sara use her own power to
heal Ricardo's heart?

Don't miss this thrilling new story in
THE CALLING *mini-series, available next*
month in Mills & Boon® Intrigue's new
NOCTURNE *series.*

Devotion Calls
by
Caridad Piñeiro

Spanish Harlem, New York City

The saints' eyes followed him as he worked, scolding him for using them for his lie. Mocking him for denying the truth about what he was.

Ricardo Fernandez paused and laid his hands on the altar that embodied the fraud that was his life. All around him the statues of the saints condemned him. But he was used to such censure from those who refused to believe in his powers. Those whose fears forced him to hide behind the guise of a *santero*.

He looked down at his hands and, as he had countless times in his thirty years of life, considered why he had been chosen to carry this burden. Why these hands, which looked just like those of any other man, possessed the power to give life or take it away.

If he was a lesser man, he might have fallen into the trap of considering himself almost godlike. He might have opted to sell his abilities to those who paid the highest price to be saved. He could have even made a perfect assassin, able to kill without leaving a trace.

But Ricardo had done none of those things. Neither regrets nor revelry had a place in his life now, so he resumed his task. With a gentle touch, he removed the offerings he had placed on the altar the day before: the fine cigar, now just a half-burned stub and a pile of ashes, and the shot glass of fragrant rum, which had nearly evaporated from the heat of the radiator just a few feet away. After checking the water level in the vase of sunflowers he had placed beside one *virgencita,* he shifted to the last offering.

A small pile of coins lay at the foot of one statue. He gathered up the money in his hand and thanked the deity. While he himself was not a true believer in Santería, his customers held to this faith and he wouldn't besmirch their tenets. He hoped his prayer was deemed respectful enough by the deities that allowed him to use the powers with which he had been born.

Ricardo didn't like living a lie, but posing as a *santero*—a priest of the Afro-Caribbean religious

Santería—was the only way he could use his healing gifts. Many of the people who sought him out might not have come to him if they realized his abilities were earthly. They preferred to think the powers came from rituals beseeching their gods.

Of course, if some god hadn't decided to give him this boon, who had? Ricardo refused to consider the alternative, since he had sworn never to use the dark side of his gift. Not even when someone asked for it.

As had happened just the other day with Evita Martinez.

He had been seeing Evita for just over a year now, ever since the doctors at one of New York City's more prestigious hospitals had told her that there was nothing else they could do for her cancer. They'd sent her home to enjoy what was left of her life.

But Evita hadn't wanted to die just yet. Having heard about his unique abilities from some of the other ladies in the neighborhood, she had come to him for help. She and her daughter, Sara.

Sara, he thought with a sigh, recalling the way she had stood before him nearly a year ago, condemning him with her body language as he talked about what he could and could not do for Evita.

He knew that Sara hadn't believed him. Worse, that she considered him a charlatan. Her bright hazel eyes had skewered him with disbelief, much like those of the saints.

The disbelief in her eyes turned to trepidation when, after finding out that she was a nurse, he had asked for payment of a most unusual kind—blood. For a moment he'd thought she might run, and take her mother with her, but then despair had crept into her eyes.

Sara loved her mother, and at that moment she had been desperate enough to do anything to help her— even if it meant bringing bags of blood to a man she considered less than dirt. Ricardo hated relying on that despair. He hated the lying, but he did what he had to so he could help people.

When Sara brought a blood bag later today, he would have to tell the prickly nurse that her mother's cancer was growing faster than he could contain it, and that Evita had asked him to help her pass peacefully when the time came, rather than suffer with the pain.

Healing and killing. His gift and his curse.

A tap sounded against the glass of his door. He turned from the altar and stared toward the front of his store.

Sara Martinez stood there, her chin tucked into the thick collar of the charcoal-gray down jacket she wore against the lingering chill of winter. A crazy gust of March wind sent her silky shoulder-length brown hair swirling around her face. With a gloved hand, she combed it back and shifted from foot to foot, impatient and intractable as always about these visits.

The early morning sun played across her pretty,

heart-shaped face. She had a hint of a cleft in her chin, and hazel eyes that expressed so much with just a look. In his case, generally disgust. But he had seen how those eyes could warm to a molten caramel when they gazed upon someone she loved.

And her lips… They were full, at least most of the time. Not when she shot him a grim look, as she did right now as she waited at his door.

Drawing a deep breath, he prepared himself to break the news that would surely devastate her.

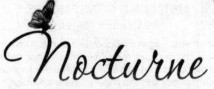

FROM INTERNATIONAL BESTSELLING AUTHOR DEBBIE MACOMBER

HIS *Winter* BRIDE

DEBBIE MACOMBER

Childhood sweethearts and unexpected romance...heading home for the holidays could lead to three winter weddings!

Available 5th December 2008

M&B

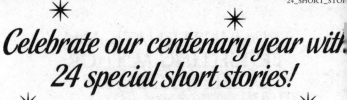

Celebrate 100 years of pure reading pleasure with Mills & Boon®

To mark our centenary, each month we're publishing a special 100th Birthday Edition. These celebratory editions are packed with extra features and include a FREE bonus story.

Plus, you have the chance to enter a fabulous monthly prize draw. See 100th Birthday Edition books for details.

Now that's worth celebrating!

September 2008

Crazy about her Spanish Boss by Rebecca Winters
Includes FREE bonus story
Rafael's Convenient Proposal

November 2008

**The Rancher's Christmas Baby
by Cathy Gillen Thacker**
Includes FREE bonus story *Baby's First Christmas*

December 2008

One Magical Christmas by Carol Marinelli
Includes FREE bonus story *Emergency at Bayside*

Look for Mills & Boon® 100th Birthday Editions at your favourite bookseller or visit
www.millsandboon.co.uk

FREE

4 BOOKS AND A SURPRISE GIFT!

We would like to take this opportunity to thank you for reading this Mills & Boon® book by offering you the chance to take FOUR more specially selected titles from the Intrigue series absolutely FREE! We're also making this offer to introduce you to the benefits of the Mills & Boon® Book Club—

- ★ FREE home delivery
- ★ FREE gifts and competitions
- ★ FREE monthly Newsletter
- ★ Books available before they're in the shops
- ★ Exclusive Mills & Boon® Book Club offers

Accepting these FREE books and gift places you under no obligation to buy; you may cancel at any time, even after receiving your free shipment. Simply complete your details below and return the entire page to the address below. You don't even need a stamp!

YES! Please send me 4 free Intrigue books and a surprise gift. I understand that unless you hear from me, I will receive 6 superb new titles every month for just £3.15 each, postage and packing free. I am under no obligation to purchase any books and may cancel my subscription at any time. The free books and gift will be mine to keep in any case.

I8ZEE

Ms/Mrs/Miss/Mr..Initials ....
BLOCK CAPITALS PLEASE

Surname ....

Address ....

....

....Postcode ....

Send this whole page to:
The Mills & Boon Book Club, FREEPOST CN81, Croydon, CR9 3WZ